the
dating
debate

Dating Dilemma Series

the *dating* debate

Dating Dilemma Series

CHRIS CANNON

Entangled Publishing, LLC
2614 South Timberline Road
Suite 105, PMB 159
Fort Collins, CO 80525
Visit our website at www.entangledpublishing.com.

Crush is an imprint of Entangled Publishing, LLC.

Edited by Erin Molta
Cover design by Bree Archer
Cover art from Shutterstock

Manufactured in the United States of America

First Edition February 2018

This book is dedicated to my family for all of their love and support even when I act like a crazy person.

Chapter One

Valentine's Day should be optional. Like, if you don't have a boyfriend or a girlfriend, the holiday should disappear. That way, single people like me wouldn't be subjected to frilly hearts and cherubs all over the place. Who came up with the idea that a baby in a diaper with a bow and arrow was romantic, anyway? It's ridiculous. The whole stupid holiday was probably a marketing ploy thought up by florists, so they could sell overpriced flowers to desperate guys who were hoping to get laid.

Maybe, if I'd ever had a boyfriend on Valentine's Day, I would feel differently. I'm sure I'm not the only seventeen-year-old girl whose favorite part of the holiday is all the chocolate that goes on sale the day after.

Which made the fact that I was balanced precariously on a ladder, trying to hang a banner for the Valentine's Dance a little ironic. "How's it look?" I shouted down to the other people who'd been drafted and put to work on the decorating committee.

"A little higher," Lisa called out.

"Define a little." I turned back to see my friend tilting her head to the right.

"Go up two inches," she said.

I shoved the sign up a little bit higher and then pushed a thumbtack into the wall.

"We're supposed to use tape," she said.

I climbed down the ladder, pretending I hadn't heard her.

"Nina, we're going to get into trouble if we use thumbtacks."

I sighed and turned to face her. "Unless you can magically pull tape out of your"—wait, we were still at school—"ear, then we're going with thumbtacks because that's all I could find."

She glanced around and then pointed to a group of girls across the gym who were working on a giant heart made of hot pink tissue paper, red ribbon, and chicken wire. "They probably have tape."

No way was I going to talk to the fashionistas. "If you want to go ask them, feel free."

"Nope." She pointed at our sign, hanging above the trophy case in the gym, which declared CUPID IS COMING. "Is it me, or does that sound like some sort of horror movie?"

I grinned. "You're not wrong. If we didn't need extra credit for home economics, I wouldn't be doing this."

"You're the one who burned our chicken pot pie in Foods class," she reminded me.

"The reason I'm in Foods class is because I don't know how to cook. Therefore, I shouldn't be penalized when the food is screwed up."

"That's your logic?" she asked.

"Yes, and I'm sticking to it." I checked the time on my cell. It was quarter after three. School had officially been over for fifteen minutes. "We've done our part. Let's get out of here."

It was Friday night, but before I could go out I had one chore to do. It was the same chore I did every day—sweep up the dog fur dust bunnies in the living room. Not that I minded, because dogs were far more agreeable than most of the people I knew. And a heck of a lot more faithful than most guys.

I was almost done when my brother, Jason, who was a year younger than me, came downstairs and dropped a bomb on my social life. I gripped the broom like a bat, and contemplated taking a swing at his head. "How could you do this to me?"

"What? I thought you wanted to go to the Valentine's Day Dance. It's all you've griped about for a week."

How could he be so stupid? There were days when I'd swear one of us was adopted. "Wrong. I griped about the stupidity of the holiday because it makes single people feel defective."

He scratched his head, looking genuinely confused. "Which is why I thought you'd be happier if you had a date."

The idiot's heart was in the right place…but still. "I never asked you to play matchmaker."

"Cole is a nice guy. He's willing to take you to the dance. What's the problem?"

"You turned me into a charity case. That's the problem."

He shook his head. "If you don't want to go to the dance, just say no when he asks. It's that simple."

But it wasn't that simple, not by a long shot, because Cole was a rare breed of guy—decent. Unfortunately, he fell firmly into the friend-zone category. Why? One day when I'd been sitting at the park reading *Harry Potter*, just blissing out in the sunshine, he sat down beside me and said he didn't understand why I'd want to read on such a nice day and that he just didn't get the big deal about *Harry Potter*. That was it. The die was cast. I couldn't date someone who didn't read, much less someone who didn't understand the fabulousness that was *Harry Potter*.

"If you see him again before I do, tell him I don't want to go to the dance."

"Nope. If you want to turn the guy down, that's on you." And then my brother walked away from me.

Now what? I checked the time. Lisa was picking me up in an hour for our Friday night Nerd Girl festivities. We go to the bookstore, *ooh* and *ah* over all the books, and then pick out a precious few to buy. Afterward, we drink frothy coffee concoctions in the cafe while we discuss how book boyfriends are so much easier to deal with than guys in real life.

I put the broom and dustpan away in the kitchen pantry. Gidget lay by her dog dish looking mildly offended. I squatted down to pet her head. "I have no idea how you're not bald." She rolled over so I could rub her tummy. Blonde fur drifted through the air and hung there, defying gravity. "It's a good thing we love you."

Gidget couldn't help the fact that she shed like a fiend. The vet said she was a yellow Lab, which for some reason meant she shed more than any other breed on the planet. She was also the sweetest dog you'd ever meet. She loved everyone. If a burglar ever broke into our house, all he'd have to do was rub her tummy and she'd happily watch him run off with all our belongings.

A knock sounded on the front door. Gidget trotted over to the front picture window and used her long nose to burrow behind the curtains so she could see who it was. The barking that followed let me know exactly who stood on my front porch. There was only one person Gidget didn't like: West

Smith, the disagreeable hottie who lived next door. He wasn't as cranky as his father, who happened to be our landlord, but he wasn't the friendly type either.

I opened the door. West stood on my front porch in jeans and a black leather coat, looking all sorts of hot and brooding. His artfully messy dark-blond hair hung down, partially obscuring his blue eyes, which would have been gorgeous except they were narrowed like he was irritated, which seemed to be his normal state.

Going for a casual demeanor, I leaned against the doorframe. "Hey, West. What's up?"

Gidget continued barking. He glared in her direction. "What did I ever do to your stupid dog?"

I crossed my arms over my chest. "Calling her stupid isn't going to win you any points."

"Well, blocking my driveway isn't going to win you any points. If you don't move your Jeep before my dad gets home, he'll probably have it towed."

"First off, we pay rent, so it's our driveway, too. And I'm not blocking your side." I may have parked right up against the bright yellow line that West's dad had made him paint down the middle of the shared cement strip, but I wasn't over it.

West glared at me. "Work with me here, Nina. My dad is driving the Humvee today. If you don't move your Jeep, he'll probably take off your driver's-side mirror and not even notice."

Wrong. His dad would probably take off my mirror on purpose. He was that special kind of jerk. "People with shared driveways should drive smaller cars."

"Feel free to explain that fact to my dad the next time you see him. For now, move your Jeep."

At that moment, my mom pulled into the driveway and parked her car, hugging the line the same way I had. The apple obviously didn't fall far from the tree. She climbed out of the car balancing a bunch of take-out boxes stacked up to her chin. I started across the lawn, but West was faster.

"Let me help you with those." He grabbed several boxes off the top of the stack.

"Thank you, West." My mom beamed at him. She seemed to be under the delusion that he was a nice young man. "China Garden had a special on shrimp fried rice. You're welcome to join us."

I could see the expression on West's face. It looked like he was trying not to roll his eyes. I decided to mess with him. "You should stay for dinner. We can discuss my plan to erase the driveway line one night and move it over about six inches."

West walked past me toward the house. "I think my father would notice that." He stopped on the front step like he wasn't sure if he was invited inside.

"You can put those in the kitchen," I said.

He went into the house and veered right, toward the table, where he deposited the containers of rice. My mother followed behind him. Gidget kept her eye on West, circling the room to stand protectively between him and my mom.

"Gidget." My mom set the rest of the food down, and then patted her on the head. "It's okay."

"There's something wrong with your dog," West said.

"She feels the same way about you," I shot back.

"On that note, I'm leaving."

The sound of a car pulling into the driveway had all of us turning to look out the kitchen window. Unless West's dad had traded in his giant gas-guzzling SUV for a red Prius, someone else had just pulled up the drive to West's house.

"Should you go see who that is?" I asked.

The way his eyebrows scrunched together told me he knew who it was, and he wasn't happy about it.

Chapter Two

What is Vicky doing here? I walked over and peered out the living room window. She sat in her car, looking at her phone. My cell beeped, which meant she'd texted me. Great.

Your car is here. I know you're home. Come talk to me.

"It's Vicky, isn't it?" Nina grinned like she knew a big secret. "Why are you hiding from your girlfriend?"

"Ex-girlfriend," I said.

"Since when?"

"It's been a few weeks." Not like I was going to share the details of my dating life with her.

"I bet she's having Valentine's Day Dance remorse."

"What does that mean?"

"She probably wants to go to the dance, and getting back together with you would be way easier than finding a new guy to take her." Nina chuckled like the situation was hilarious.

"Not funny." Vicky had seen my car. What could I do? "I'm texting that I'm having dinner with my neighbors."

All three of us watched as Vicky looked to the right at Nina's house and then to the left at the empty lot that separated my house from the neighbors on the other side.

"What's everyone watching?" Jason, Nina's brother, asked as he came into the room. Our paths had crossed at school a few times. He was a decent guy.

"Hey, West."

"Hello," I said. "My ex, Vicky, stopped by. I think she's coming over here. You should ask her to the Valentine's Dance."

"No thanks. I like my life drama free." He walked over to the table, filled a plate with fried rice, and leaned back against the counter. "I'll just stay and watch the show."

Apparently, everyone in this house was a smart-ass.

Vicky approached the front door and knocked.

"Let's all play nice," Nina's mom said as she walked over to open the door. "Hello, can I help you?"

"Is West here? Can I speak to him?"

"Sure. We were just sitting down to dinner." Her mom stepped back so Vicky could see me. "Would you like to join us for some fried rice?"

What in the hell was her mother trying to do?

"No, thanks." Vicky gave a polite smile. "Sorry to barge in during dinner. West, can we talk?"

There was no easy way out of this, but I had no intention of entertaining Nina's family with my life any more than I already had. "Sure. Let's go sit on my back patio where we'll have some privacy." It was barely fifty degrees outside, so that should help keep the conversation short.

"Okay."

We went out the front door and around the side of the house. I opened the gate into the backyard and headed over to sit at the umbrella table. Since I didn't know why she was here, I waited for her to start talking.

"I know we broke up, but my mom bought a Valentine's dress for me, and she expects me to wear it to the dance, whether I have a date or not." Vicky ducked her head. "Going without a date would be awkward. Not like this conversation isn't, but I was hoping we could go as friends?" She glanced up with a hopeful look on her face.

Before I could answer, another car pulled up the driveway. "It's like Grand Central Station around here tonight."

"Is that Cole Harris?" Vicky asked. "What's he doing here?"

He headed toward Nina's front door.

"And why is Nina creeping out her back door like some sort of spy?" Vicky asked.

Nina ducked low, like she didn't want anyone inside to see her through the back window, and then ran over to join us. "I'm going to hide over here for a while, if you two don't mind."

"Why are you hiding from Cole?" I asked.

"My brother told him to ask me on a date."

"You don't want to go out with him?" Vicky said. "Why? What's wrong with him?"

"Nothing. He's a great guy, but he's never read *Harry Potter*." Nina stated this like it was a crime against humanity.

I tilted my head and studied her.

"What?" she asked.

"I'm trying to figure out if you're Ginny or Hermione."

"I'm pretty sure you're Draco," she replied.

"There you are," Jason called from across the backyard with Cole by his side.

"I am going to suffocate my brother in his sleep," Nina said as she smiled and waved.

I laughed.

"I'm not joking," she said. Cole and her brother crossed the backyard to join us. "Hey, Cole. I didn't know you were here."

"I stopped by because I wanted to ask you something." The poor guy looked at the small crowd of people and seemed to reconsider his mission. "Nina, can we talk over at your house, maybe?"

"Actually, there was something I wanted to ask you." Nina pointed at Vicky. "Do you know Vicky? She and West used to date."

Cole nodded. "Sure. Hello, Vicky."

Vicky smiled. "Hello."

"The Valentine's Dance is coming up," Nina said, "and the last I heard you weren't seeing anyone, so I think you and Vicky should go to the dance together."

Cole tilted his head and looked at Nina like he didn't quite understand the situation. "You want me to ask *Vicky* to the dance?"

Nina nodded like this was a fabulous idea.

She seemed to enjoy throwing people off-balance. Maybe it was time someone did it to her.

"Since Nina and I are going to the dance, it makes sense that you'd ask Vicky."

Chapter Three

"You're going to the dance with West?" Cole said like he didn't quite believe it.

If I wasn't before, I sure as hell was now, if for no other reason than to wipe the smug smile off West's obnoxiously handsome face. "Yes. Yes, I am. He just asked me. Isn't that the funniest thing?"

Cole looked around at all of us like he wasn't sure if we were telling the truth or lying through our teeth. Vicky cleared her throat and smiled at him.

He shrugged. "Okay then. Vicky, do you want to go to the dance?"

"I'd love to," she said. "Why don't we go grab a hot chocolate somewhere so we can talk."

"Sure." He followed her out to their cars.

Jason looked at me and then at West like he was trying to figure something out. After a minute, he shrugged like he didn't understand and didn't really care. "Food's getting cold." He headed back to our house.

"He's right." Plus I was freezing, since I hadn't stopped to grab my coat. "Let's go talk about the dance over fried rice."

"We're not actually going to the dance," West said.

Oh, how wrong he was. "Nope. You said it. You put it out into the universe that we were going to the dance, so we're going."

"Now you sound like Luna Lovegood."

I laughed and ran back over to my house. The fact that West was fluent in *Harry Potter* made him even more attractive than he'd been before.

He didn't follow immediately, but something told me he would, just to argue his case. I'd been keeping an eye on West since we moved in, spinning fantasies in my head about the hot, brooding son of the landlord falling for the hippy-chick bookworm renting the house next door to him. Not that I thought it would ever happen, but hey, a girl can dream.

Back in the kitchen, I grabbed a carton of fried rice and ate straight from the box.

My mom pointed at the dishes she'd set on the table. "Use a plate."

Jason had ditched the plate he'd used earlier and was eating straight from a box, as he sat on the couch watching television. I'm not sure why I had to use a plate. It wasn't worth arguing about, so I did as she asked. "Surprise plot twist in my life," I told my mom. "West asked me to the Valentine's Dance."

"That sounds like fun," she said. "Do we need to go shopping for a dress?"

I loathed shopping. Normally, I felt pretty good about myself. But nothing made me feel chunky and pale like trying on clothes under fluorescent lights in front of full-length mirrors. "No. I'm sure I have something I can wear."

"Come in," I heard Jason shout from the other room.

West came walking into the kitchen, his fabulous blue eyes laser focused on me. "We should talk."

"You should eat," my mom said, shoving a carton at him. She stood and wiped her hands with a napkin. "I have a hot date with a book. I'll see you two later."

"So reading runs in the family," West said.

"Yes. Except for my brother. I'm 60 percent sure he's adopted."

"So, this whole dance thing?" West picked up a fork, took a bite of rice, and stared at me like he was waiting for me to give him an easy out. Not going to happen. Mess with a smart girl and suffer the consequences.

"You started it," was the most amusing response I could come up with.

"No." He shook his head as if trying to emphasize his response. "You started it when you invited me in for dinner."

"Why? Because I knew you'd rather eat dirt than join us for rice? That's your fault for being a suck-up and carrying my mom's food."

"I was being nice," he shot back.

"No good deed goes unpunished." I batted my eyelashes at him. "Besides, I was going to help her before you rushed over."

He looked at me like I was crazy. "So I shouldn't have helped your mom, but it's okay for you to shove Cole off on Vicky."

"Please. He's a nice guy. She'll fall for him...maybe because he's the total opposite of you."

He pointed his fork at me. "Where do you get off judging me?"

"I'm not judging you. I meant you're all black-leather-jacket-brooding loner guy, and he's Mr.-Happy-Sunshine-everyone-is-my-friend."

"Fine. Mr. Sunshine is out of the way now, so there's no

need for us to go to the dance."

"Nice try," I said. "We're going to the dance."

"Why?"

"Because you said we were," I said. "And lying is never acceptable. Don't stress about this. I'm not proposing we run off to Mexico and get matching his-and-her tattoos. We'll just go to the dance together. No big deal."

"Right. Nothing is ever that simple."

I walked over to the cabinet and pulled out two mini Hershey bars. I held one out to him. "While I *am* enjoying this argument, I have to cut it short."

He looked at the chocolate bar and then back at my face. "What?"

"Oh dear." I smiled. "I've confused you. Allow me to recap. I like debating. The chocolate is for you because all meals should end in chocolate, and I have to go because I'm going to the bookstore."

He made no move to accept the chocolate, so I placed it in his shirt pocket and patted his chest...because why not. "There you go."

"You're insane."

"My brother has tried that argument. He always loses. Quick question. Do you read mostly paper or ebook?"

"Do you try to give people conversational whiplash? Or are you incapable of maintaining a topic?"

Be still my heart, he's playing my game. "If a person can't keep up, they should consider upping their caffeine consumption." I smiled at him. "Now back to my question. Paper or digital?"

"I read almost everything on my Kindle or my cell."

"I love my Kindle, but I like paper books, too. Sometimes, I buy the paper books to keep on my shelf and read the ebook instead."

"Why?"

"What if there's an EMP blast that destroys all digital content? You'd have nothing to read. And that would be a true apocalypse scenario. Plus, I like the way books smell."

"Right. I'm going to take my rice and go. Have fun buying things that will collect dust on your shelves."

"So negative. You should try to relax."

Chapter Four

WEST

Time for me to make my escape. Nina might be cute and funny, but she was oddly confrontational. I didn't need that in my life. I didn't need her judging me, or her crazy dog barking at me.

There was a reason Gidget didn't like me. She saw what I did late at night in the backyard. Thank God dogs couldn't talk, or I'd be in a world of trouble. Sometimes, you had to take things into your own hands, but I wasn't sure the fire department or my father would see it that way.

My cell buzzed with a text. It was my dad. Great. He was working late and wanted me to make sure to fix dinner for my mom. I glanced at the boxes of fried rice. "Since you have so much, I'm going to take an extra box for my mom."

"You have a mom?"

"Everyone has a mom," I said.

"Touché." She nodded like she was awarding me a point. "What I meant was I didn't know your mom lived with you.

I've never seen her."

Time to spin my well-practiced web of lies. "She doesn't leave the house much."

"Why not?"

"She's sick, and I don't like to talk about it."

"Oh." Her demeanor changed from captain of the debate team to a concerned, normal person. "I'm sorry. Is there anything I can do to help?"

"No."

"I could bring her some books," Nina said.

Like I'd said earlier, nothing was ever simple. I pulled out the line that usually made people uncomfortable enough to back off. "The doctors say it's best to keep visitors and outside items to a minimum due to her condition."

Nina reached over and put her hand on my forearm. "I'm so sorry."

"Thanks." I stood, intent on avoiding any more questions, but I needed to make sure she wouldn't just pop over. "What's your number?"

She rattled off her cell number. I dialed it to make sure she'd have my number in her phone. "If, for some random reason you want to get ahold of me, like if you come to your senses and realize we aren't going to the dance, text or call. Don't come over to my house and knock, ever, because you might wake up my mom."

"Is that why your dad wants us to put the rent check in that weird mailbox on the shed?"

"That, plus he's antisocial." No reason to lie about that. They'd met the man.

"Okay, then. I'll go with the not-waking-your-mom-up reason because that makes a lot more sense. There's one more thing before you go." She held her arms out. "You're getting a hug whether you want one or not."

Not happening. I tried to walk around her. "That's not

necessary."

She blocked my path. "If you argue, I'll call my mom in here and she'll insist on hugging you, too. We're a hugging family. It's what we do."

"You can't argue with someone and then hug them."

"Yes, I can."

She didn't seem to be backing down. "I don't need or want a hug."

"Right. Your dad acts like former military, and you just told me your mom was ill."

She stood there holding her arms out.

"Don't you have to get to the bookstore?"

"Don't worry. I've done this before." She moved in and put her arms around me, squeezing me tight. And she wasn't trying to put a move on me, which was mildly insulting.

"I won't stop hugging until you hug me back," she warned.

"You're one of the strangest people I've ever met." I hugged her back, which wasn't a hardship. After all, she was soft and warm and smelled nice.

After a few seconds, she released me and stepped away. "I prefer to think of myself as interesting. Don't forget your rice."

No way was I letting her get the last word in. "Why did your mom buy so much food? And why just shrimp fried rice? Most people buy a variety."

"No matter what else she buys we fight over the shrimp fried rice, so that's all she bothers with now. And she overbuys because she likes to feed people. It's a nurturing thing."

"I guess that goes along with hugging?" I said. "Does she like to argue with people, too?"

"No, but anyone who walks in the door will more than likely be fed and hugged. So, fair warning."

There were worse things in the world. "Maybe you should have that printed on a welcome mat so people won't be surprised." I grabbed the cartons of rice, and that's when I noticed Gidget lying by the front door. "Your dog isn't giving me the evil eye anymore."

"She saw that I trusted you, so now she probably trusts you, too."

"Okay. This has been interesting. We're not going to the dance, and I'll see you later."

She laughed. "Yes, you're wrong, and of course we will because we live next door to each other."

Nina followed me to the front door and closed it behind me.

What a bizarre day. I crossed over the shared driveway through the yard to my front door. I opened it with my key, being careful not to swing the door too wide, so I wouldn't knock anything over. After making sure it was locked behind me, I walked down the narrow path between the boxes my mother had filled and stacked floor to ceiling in the entryway and the living room. You couldn't even see the furniture anymore because it was buried under all the boxes. Even though my father had insisted on putting everything in Rubbermaid containers, the smell of mildew and dust permeated the air.

Once I hit the hallway to the kitchen, the smell faded but didn't completely go away. I opened the window above the sink and turned on the small desk fan that sat in front of it to encourage air movement.

Our kitchen still looked fairly normal since my dad refused to let my mom bring anything into it because of the possible fire hazard. I dumped rice into a bowl for my mom and set it on the table. Then I grabbed a soda from the refrigerator and drank half of it. *Okay. I can do this.* Steeling myself, I entered the hallway that led to her bedroom and wedged myself through the slender opening, which was all that was left of her doorway. "Hello, Mom."

She smiled at me like all was right in her world. Like she wasn't sitting on a pile of twisted-up bed sheets surrounded by storage tubs stacked one on top of another, lining the walls and taking up most of the rest of the room except for a small perimeter around the bed and closet. "Hello, sweetie. How was your day?"

"Good. I brought you some shrimp fried rice for dinner. It's in the kitchen."

"Oh." She played with the edge of the frayed blanket in her lap. "Can't you just bring it in here?"

"No." I'd learned not to argue. "It's waiting for you on the table."

She stood, hugging a pillow to her chest. "Can I take one pillow?"

"Sure, Mom." I backed out, turned around, and was relieved when I heard her following after me. We sat at the glass-top table, and I braced myself in preparation for the awkward small talk I felt obligated to make.

"I saw you, out the window," my mom said.

That was new. "What did you see?"

"You were talking to the daughter of the renter next door." She pointed toward their house like I wouldn't know who she was referring to.

"Her name is Nina."

"Do you like her?" my mom asked.

"Her family is odd." I laughed. "Just a different kind of odd from ours."

She reached across the table and laid her hand on top of mine, giving it a quick squeeze. "I know your dad seems rigid in his beliefs sometimes, but he always has your best interests at heart."

My father. Right. He's the problem. "I know."

She ate a few bites of rice. "I'd like to meet Nina. You should invite her over for dinner one night."

Not going to happen for the obvious reasons. Plus, she'd probably start an argument and then insist on hugging everyone. "Dad wouldn't like that."

"I know the house is a bit of a mess." She pushed her hair behind her ear, like she was suddenly self-conscious of her appearance. "I guess we could straighten up a little bit."

With a backhoe and Dumpster, maybe. "Let's put that plan on hold until I decide if I even like her, okay?"

Chapter Five

NINA

I sat at the cafe in the back of the bookstore, drinking a caramel macchiato while Lisa looked at me bug-eyed. "Oh my God. You're dating West? The brooding hottie of Greenbrier High School?"

I wiped whipped cream off my upper lip. "It's not like we're actually dating."

"It's not like you're not dating," Lisa said.

"Interesting way to look at it. So I'm not not-dating West, which makes me not-not his girlfriend, which sounds like some sort of double speak from a dystopian novel."

"It does," she said, "and I can't believe he's fluent in *Harry Potter*."

"I'm sure anyone living in that house needs the escapism of books." I told her about West's mom. "I never knew he had a mom, much less that she was ill. I guess he doesn't tell a lot of people."

"So I won't share," Lisa said.

"His house doesn't sound like a fun place to live," I said.

"Your house is like a hippie commune by comparison. I bet it drives his antisocial dad crazy."

"We're probably the calmest renters he could find," I said.

Lisa nodded. "Bookworm hippies aren't known for destroying property."

"As long as you leave our books alone and don't interrupt our flow of coffee and chocolate, we are a peaceful bunch."

"Speaking of chocolate." Lisa grabbed her wallet from her purse. "I think it's cookie time." She stood and headed back up to the counter. A few minutes later, she returned with a heart-shaped Rice Krispies Treat decorated with pink and red M&M's.

"That is not a cookie."

"I don't understand your prejudice against Rice Krispies Treats. They're yummy, and this one has chocolate in it." She plucked out an M&M and popped it into her mouth.

"It's a glorified cereal bar."

"No one said you had to eat any."

I grabbed my purse and pulled out a mini-chocolate bar. "Thankfully, I brought my own chocolate."

After we finished our food and drinks, we paid for our books and left the store.

• • •

Saturday morning, I woke up to the delicious scent of fried dough. Downstairs, I found my mom making cinnamon doughnuts out of canned biscuits.

"Those smell wonderful." I poured myself a glass of milk. "Any of them cool enough to eat?"

"Not yet." My mom used a slotted spoon to dip out the golden puffy balls and dropped them into a shallow bowl of cinnamon and sugar. "Roll those for me."

"Sure." I coated the golden brown balls and then transferred them to another plate to cool.

"So how'd things go with West yesterday?"

"Pretty good. I think we could end up friends, if nothing else."

"He seems like he could use some friends," my mom said. "That is one uptight household."

Should I tell my mom? "You can't tell Jason, but I think I know why West and his dad are so…off-putting."

"Your brother won't tell—"

"I know you gave birth to him, and you love him, and so do I, but he is not to be trusted with sensitive information." I'd never forgiven my brother for telling the entire world that I changed my eleventh birthday party from a pool party to a backyard barbecue because I'd gotten my period.

"Fine."

"West didn't give me any details, but it sounds like his mom is housebound and can't have guests because of germs."

"That's terrible." My mom set the slotted spoon down. "Is there anything we can do?"

"No, but it does explain the antisocial vibe that emanates from their house."

"That makes my heart hurt." My mom picked up the spoon and scooped out more doughnuts. "You realize I'm going to have to try to find a way to help them."

"Yeah, I've been spinning that problem around in my head since he told me. And fair warning, no knocking on their door because it might wake his mom up."

"So, no stopping over for coffee or dropping off cookies… There has to be something we can do."

I picked up one of the cinnamon sugar donuts and blew on it before popping it into my mouth. *Yum.* "Let me know if you figure something out, but don't do anything without talking to me first, okay?"

"I wouldn't want to mess things up for you." She went back to making doughnuts. "When we first signed the lease and moved in, I thought his dad was a single parent, like me. I had hoped we might bond over raising kids alone."

Uh-oh. "Please tell me you didn't hit on West's dad."

She laughed. "I might have tried if he'd ever given me the time of day, but he made it quite clear that he wasn't interested in talking to me, except to remind me that I needed to pay the rent on time."

"He's definitely not a social guy. But hey, being a single parent isn't all bad, right?"

"No, and considering I've ended up happier than your father, I feel like I've won the game of life, even if I didn't end up where I thought I'd be."

My dad was an over-the-road trucker, so it was natural that he was gone for long periods of time. What wasn't natural was the fact that he had another wife and family two states away. A midlife crisis wife, as my mom liked to refer to Sheila, since she was ten years younger than him. He'd lived a double life long enough to have a four-year-old and a two-year-old before my mom figured out what was going on.

I didn't understand why he thought he needed another family, why we hadn't been enough. It was bad enough that he cheated on my mom, but the fact that he'd created a whole other family...that cut deep.

He'd been gone so much of the time that having him completely cut from our lives didn't take much getting used to. At least that's what I told myself.

"Heard anything from him lately?" I liked to think that he might miss us.

"He's broken up about Sheila leaving him," my mom said. "And he's annoyed that I'm happy, which works for me."

So nothing about Jason or me. That sucked. "Do you think you'd ever trust a guy enough to get married again?"

Because from my viewpoint, marriage was a lost cause.

She picked up one of the donuts that had cooled off and took a bite. She chewed and stared off into the distance like she was really thinking about the question. "I'd be happy to date someone if I happened to find the right guy, but I have no desire to pick up after a man ever again. No matter how wonderful a guy may be, all males seem to be missing the gene that tells them the dirty socks are supposed to go in the hamper, rather than on the floor."

My brother performed that same maneuver. Maybe I'd give him crap about it in an effort to help his future wife. My mind shifted to West. I bet all the socks in his house landed in the hamper. His dad had probably painted a square designating exactly where the hamper had to sit.

"Are you doing anything with West today?" my mom asked.

"Not unless he asks. It's two weeks until the Valentine's Dance. I suspect he'll look for an easy out before then."

"Why do you say that?"

I didn't know him well enough to think he'd keep his word, but I couldn't tell my mom that. "I don't know. I think he was joking when he asked me to the dance. I don't want to force him to take me, if he doesn't want to go."

"Wrong." My mom sounded adamant. "He needs to stick to his commitments. You may not end up dating him for long, but he needs to learn that he can't duck his responsibilities. You'll be doing his future wife a favor."

"Like someone should have done with dad?" I asked.

"Yes." She frowned. "Exactly like that."

The worst part about my dad's defection is that none of us had seen it coming. He and my mom had seemed so happy together. I'd thought we were the perfect family. Turns out, I'd been living the perfect lie.

Chapter Six

"Big plans for Saturday night?" my dad asked as he handed me the kitchen trash bag to carry outside.

"Not sure yet." I exited through the glass patio doors and carried the bag to the trash cans on the side of the house. We'd learned the hard way that if we put the trash in the garage, my mom tried to sneak it back inside. Two-week-old garbage sealed in a plastic storage box had a gag-inducing stink all its own, which was also why we locked the garbage bins. I worked the combination lock that held the metal bar in place over the trash can lids. After disposing of the trash, I shut the lock and spun the dial, tugging on it to make sure it was closed.

Back in the kitchen my dad poured himself a cup of coffee and leaned against the counter. "I think your mom and I will watch a movie tonight."

He said this like it wasn't the same thing they did every night. I'd given up on trying to get them to leave the house.

He'd been antisocial before my mother went around the bend. Since then, it had only become worse. "If you need anything while I'm out, text me."

"Thanks." He stirred sugar into his coffee. "Anything else I should know about?"

Talk about a loaded question. "School is good."

He waited and sipped his coffee. Sometimes I wondered if he had surveillance cameras installed around the house, and he was waiting for me to confess something. On the off chance he did, I fessed up. "I talked to the neighbors."

He set his coffee down and sighed. "We discussed this."

I rushed in to explain. "It's not a big deal. I told Nina that Mom is sick and housebound so no visitors or gifts. I warned her never to stop by and knock on the door because it might wake Mom up. It's not like Nina and I are dating. We just talked. I even gave her my number so she can text or call me. No surprise visits. I promise."

"I don't like it," my dad said. "But what's done is done." He stood and headed for the hallway. "I'm going to read the paper."

That went better than I expected. I pulled out my cell and texted my cousins, Matt and Charlie. They were pretty much my best friends, my only friends, really, because they knew about my mom, which meant I didn't have to lie or keep my guard up around them. We planned to meet at the movies in a few hours.

. . .

I pulled up to the four-way stop in front of the multiplex and watched the people swarming through the parking lot. Had a movie ended or was everyone arriving? As I turned into the parking lot, a stream of cars started backing out of their spots. I found a spot near the front row and looked around for Matt and Charlie. I checked my cell. The show didn't start for another forty minutes, so they probably weren't here yet. I'd left my house as early as possible, something I always did, which made me feel guilty. But pretty much everything made me feel guilty when it came to my mom and her hoarding, so what did it matter?

I texted Matt and Charlie that I was in the parking lot, since their dad had finally relented and given them cell phones for Christmas. Before that, he'd refused to pay for them. I guess every family has its quirks. Mine were just Olympic-level compared to everyone else's.

I read a book on my cell while I waited for them to text me. Fifteen minutes later my cell buzzed. I met them in the lobby.

• • •

The show was crowded, so we ended up going halfway up before finding three seats together. Not that I cared. I never understood people like my father who had to sit in a certain spot. Not that he went to the movies much anymore. As long as I could see the screen, I didn't care.

I checked out the people seated around us. There was a familiar brown ponytail in front of me and to the left. She glanced over her shoulder and saw me. Smiling, she gave a small wave and then turned back around.

"Who's that?" Charlie asked. "She looks familiar."

"Nobody," I said. "She lives in the rental house next door."

"And?" Matt asked.

"And nothing." I didn't need them busting my balls over this.

"She did the cute little wave thing," Charlie said. "That means she's interested."

"Did you read that in your how-to-know-what-girls-are-thinking book?" I asked.

"No." Charlie laughed. "But if a guy ever wrote that he'd be rich."

"Dating your neighbor seems kind of lazy," Matt said.

"Or convenient," Charlie shot back. "Depending on how you look at it."

"We're not dating. She's not my type."

Charlie leaned over, trying to see her. "She's cute in a hippy-chick kind of way."

"Hippy chick?" I snorted.

Matt laughed.

Charlie punched me on the shoulder. "You know what I mean."

The previews came on glaringly loud, saving me from any further conversation about Nina.

• • •

We went for pizza after the show. I scanned the area for Nina but didn't see her, which was a relief. I didn't need her becoming too friendly and complicating my already complicated life. I needed to find a way out of the stupid Valentine's Day Dance and be done with her.

I glanced around the restaurant looking for an uncomplicated girl who didn't live next door to me. There were a few possibilities, but nobody that stood out. Funny, but Cole and Vicky sat together at a table across the room. They seemed to be having a good time.

"So Vicky's moved on?" Matt said.

I nodded and grabbed another slice of sausage and pepperoni pizza.

"She always seemed sort of pushy," said Charlie.

"That was one of our problems. She asked too many

questions."

Charlie and Matt made eye contact, and then they both looked at me. "How's your mom?" Matt asked.

"The same," I said.

"Have anything you need us to drop off at Goodwill?" Charlie asked.

"Yeah, I have a couple of boxes in the shed out back."

At eleven thirty, they followed me back to the house. Working as quietly as possible, we loaded three cardboard boxes into the back of their pickup truck. The boxes were filled with old dishes and clothes my mom had picked up at garage sales back when she used to leave the house. I collected random items I could sneak out of the house a little bit at a time, and Charlie and Matt took care of them for me. This didn't begin to put a dent into my mom's collection, but at least it felt like I was doing something.

Chapter Seven

NINA

Monday morning at school, I was surprised to find Cole waiting by my locker. "Hey, Cole. What's up?"

"I wanted to thank you for introducing me to Vicky. She's great."

"I'm glad you two hit it off." And I meant it. He was a good guy, despite the fact that he didn't understand the *Harry Potter* fandom.

"Since you and West are the reason we met, Vicky thinks we should go on a double date."

"She does?" Because that was kind of odd. Why would she want to double with her ex? "I'll mention it to him."

He nodded like he'd accomplished his mission and then walked off.

"You're dating West?" A girl two lockers down who was a known gossip moved closer to me with a sly look on her face. Great. News of my non-relationship was going to make the rounds of Greenbrier High before the end of the day.

"It's nothing official," I said, trying to throw her off the scent. "No big deal."

"Don't you live next door to him?" she asked, like it was some sort of conspiracy.

"I do."

"So are you like neighbors with benefits?" the girl asked.

Seriously? "No. No we are not. He asked me to the Valentine's Dance. That's it. No benefits involved at this point in time."

The bell rang, and I headed to homeroom, making a mental note to find West as soon as possible to make sure he understood that the neighbors with benefits story, while entertaining, was not to be encouraged.

I sat near Lisa in first hour and filled her in on my strange morning.

"Why would Vicky want to go on a double date?" Lisa asked. "Unless she's being passive-aggressive. And the neighbors thing? That's ridiculous."

"Agreed."

• • •

By lunch, enough people had given me the side-eye that I wanted to track the gossiping girl down and strangle her with the strap of her neon pink backpack. Not that I gave a crap what people thought, most of the time, but lies really ticked me off.

Lisa and I sat at our normal table in the smart girl/ bookworm section of the cafeteria. West usually sat a few tables away, bordering the cool kid section, but today he walked past his table and came to sit with me.

"Not that I mind, but what prompted this lunchtime visit?"

He smiled. "I'm going to go out on a limb and guess you're

not the one telling people we've been sleeping together since you moved in next door and that's why Vicky and I broke up."

"What?" I ripped open my bag of Cheez-Its with a little too much force, and they went flying in all directions. *Why are people so stupid?* "Nope. Wasn't me." I gathered up the Cheez-Its that landed on my sandwich and my napkin and put them back in the bag. The ones that had landed on the table were now suspect, so I shoved them in a pile off to the side.

"Did you tell anyone anything?" he asked. "Because I don't think Vicky would start that kind of rumor."

"I mentioned to someone that we were neighbors."

"Maybe she thought you were speaking in code," Lisa teased.

"Not funny." I flicked one of the contaminated Cheez-Its at her. "Speaking of Vicky, did you hear she wants us to go on a double date with her and Cole?"

"No way," he said. "I broke up with her, which means I don't have to deal with her anymore." He pointed at me and then back at himself. "And we are not dating."

"Did you really think you needed to clarify who you were talking about with a gesture? There are only three of us here, and I love Lisa, but not in a let's-shack-up-and-raise-poodles sort of way."

"I just wanted to be clear." He pushed his chair away from the table.

"We're still going to the dance," I told him.

"No. We're not," he said.

"Yes we are, because otherwise I lied when I agreed with you," I said.

"So?"

"I don't lie," I said.

"Never?"

"No. I think you should always tell the truth, no matter

how painful it is."

West looked at me like he didn't believe me. He checked out the people at surrounding tables. "See that girl over my shoulder who looks like she put on her makeup with a spatula?"

I nodded. "What about her?"

"If she asked how you liked her new makeup, what would you say?"

"I'd say her lipstick is a pretty color and then suggest she might want to wear a little less eye makeup during the day."

"Which means you'd avoid telling her the truth," West said. "Which is the same as lying."

"No. It's not. We're going to the dance. End of story."

"Why?" He scooted his chair back toward the table. "Seriously. Why do you want to go to the Valentine's Dance with me?"

I didn't. Not really. "Whether I want to go with you or not, doesn't matter."

"So you don't want to go with me?" He tilted his head and studied me.

"It's not you that I don't want to go with."

He closed his eyes like he was trying to figure something out. "Does what you're saying actually make sense to you?"

"Of course it does. It's not that I don't want to go with you. I don't want to go with anyone. Valentine's Day is a stupid tradition. Valentine's Day dances doubly so."

"If it's stupid, then why are you insisting we go?"

"Karma, truth, justice, and the American way. Take your pick. You said we were going, so we're going."

"Isn't there some guy out there with a huge library you'd rather spend your time with?"

"Awww." I patted him on the shoulder. "Are you insecure about the size of your library? I'm sure it's fine."

West glared at me. And then he stood up and walked

over to where he normally sat.

"Well, that was entertaining," Lisa said. "What do you think the odds are of him taking you to the dance?"

"Who knows?" While I was sure I wasn't his dream date, I wasn't a troll. There were worse things than going to the Valentine's Dance with your stubborn, argumentative, bookworm neighbor. I'd do my best to convince him of that. If it came down to a battle of wills, I was pretty sure I could out-debate him and outlast him in the stubbornness department.

Chapter Eight

Vicky approached me at my locker after school. Before she could get a word out, I said, "The answer is no. We're not going on a double date."

"Well, that's rude," she said.

"No. It's normal." I slung my bag over my shoulder. "People don't go on double dates with their exes."

"You're taking this all wrong. I really like Cole."

"Good for you. Be happy with him and stop tormenting me." I slammed my locker and turned to go.

"So are you and Nina a couple, because I heard the strangest rumor."

I turned back around. "No, you heard a stupid rumor."

"Same thing, really." She grinned like this was all a big joke.

"Vicky, bottom line, what do you want?"

"For all of us to be friends," she said.

"I doubt that."

"Honestly, you were a bad boyfriend."

"Thanks for clearing that up." I turned to walk away from her.

"But I still care about you, and you need friends," she said.

That brought me up short. I turned back to her. "I have friends. And you're not one of them." The look of hurt on her face made me regret my words. Whatever. It was too late now. I headed for my car.

Honestly. Did she have delusions of being a social worker or a psychiatrist? I had more than enough friends. Adding people to my life never made it simpler. They always asked too many questions, just like Vicky had.

As I drove home, I wondered why I'd even bothered with her. She was pretty and curvy, but none of that made up for the lectures about how I should act or how weird it was that she could never come inside my house. Like I didn't know that was weird, but facts were facts. Until I moved out of my parents' home, I'd continue to protect my mom's secret. I planned to move out as soon as possible. I'd received acceptance letters from most of the schools I'd applied to. Now I was waiting to hear back about their financial aid packages. If all went according to plan, I'd trade my grade point average in for a scholarship to a university far away from Greenbrier.

When I pulled into our shared driveway, I noticed Nina had beaten me home and parked right on the edge of the line, again. I parked on my side, behind her so I didn't have to deal with making sure our driver's-side and passenger-side mirrors didn't hit. Why couldn't my dad have rented to some conservationists who drove tiny little smart cars?

No. He'd rented to Nina's family. Nina—oddly interesting and sexy in a smart-girl kind of way, who tried to turn everything into a debate or a confrontation. As entertaining as she might be, I didn't need any more conflict in my life.

And it's not like she wanted to go to the stupid dance anyway. It was all about the truth. What I needed was to find a way to catch her in a lie, and then she couldn't pretend to be so high and mighty about always telling the truth.

I put my car in park and sat, taking in the view. To the right, I could see inside Nina's house because the curtains were open. There was light and movement. My house sat there like a tomb, quiet and sealed. The curtains were shut tight. No light or air moved through the house. My mom probably sat in the middle of her bed like a deranged bird on a crazy nest of bedsheets that needed to be washed.

The weight of it all pushed down on me. I wasn't ready to go in yet, but I knew my mom would be waiting for me. If I was late, she'd get worked up. I checked the calendar on my phone. Only 120 days until graduation. I could do this.

I went into the house and started a pot of French roast. Once it was ready, I poured two cups and added sugar to both, leaving them on the table. If the smell didn't lure my mom out of her room, I'd go get her. In the meantime, I made a PB&J and ate it while I made another two sandwiches, which I cut into fourths and put on a plate.

This was how my mom used to greet me when I came home from school as a kid. Back then, my cup had been full of milk, but I still found the routine comforting, and I think she did, too.

I heard footsteps. My mom came around the corner. "That smells wonderful."

She sat and sipped her coffee. It was funny, but at times like these she seemed like a normal person, like her old self.

"How was your day?" she asked.

"Pretty good," I said. "How about you?"

She picked up a sandwich square. "I cleaned out some boxes today."

The bite I'd taken seemed to lodge in my throat. After

taking a drink of coffee, I worked at keeping my tone even. "Really? What did you do?"

"I'll show you after we eat."

"Okay."

"I know your dad doesn't like it when I move things around, but I wasn't sure where my magazines were."

She had three giant tubs of magazines in the bedroom, which my father had clearly labeled with a large black permanent marker. "Weren't they in the right boxes?"

"It's hard to find them when they're in the boxes," she said.

"If you didn't keep so many of them, you'd be able to find the ones you wanted."

"Let me show you what I did." She stood and headed for her bedroom.

I checked the time on my cell. My dad wouldn't be home for an hour and a half. Hopefully, I had time to fix whatever she'd done.

I walked in the doorway of her bedroom and leaned against the doorframe, praying for strength. She'd taken all the magazines out and stacked them on the dresser. There had to be hundreds of them. The stacks were so tall you couldn't see the mirror. She'd also piled them on the floor in the space that had been left as a walkway to the closet.

I ran my hand down my face and worked at keeping my tone even. "Dad won't like this. We need to put them back in the boxes."

"Let me worry about your father," she said.

Right. Like it was that simple. "Why don't you pick out your favorite magazines, and I'll put the rest in the recycling bin."

"There's no way I could choose," my mom said. "I need all of them."

If I argued, she'd become agitated, so I tried another

tactic. "Do you have any car magazines? Charlie said he and Matt were looking at cars."

"I do have some car magazines." She brightened and went over to the stacks on the dresser. After a few minutes, she came back holding a dozen *Car and Driver* magazines. "See, this is why I never throw anything away, because you never know when you might need it."

"Thanks, Mom, I'm sure Charlie and Matt will appreciate them." I held my hand out.

She stared at the magazines and then at my hand. Retreating a step, she hugged the magazines to her chest. "Tell them they can come here and read them. That way I won't lose them."

Why had I thought that might work? Time to retreat. "Sure. I'm going to start on my homework now."

"Okay." My mom went back to her bed, still clutching the magazines.

I didn't actually feel like doing homework, so I headed into the living room and shifted a few boxes so I could climb over them toward the middle of the room. That way, if my mom wandered in, she wouldn't be able to spot me right away. I opened a tub and filled an old backpack with junk mail that had to be at least five years old. When another sliver of paper wouldn't fit inside, I snuck back out, grabbed my coat, and went out the sliding glass patio doors into the backyard.

I crept across the patio, through the grass, and out past the shed to an old overgrown basketball court that the former owners of the house had installed, which my dad never had any use for. I kept an old barbecue grill and a couple of lawn chairs on the cracked concrete slab for plausible deniability. I opened the grill and dumped the old mail inside. From the cooler I kept near the grill, I pulled out a container of lighter fluid. After dousing the papers, I threw a few charcoal briquettes on top and then tossed in a match. The lighter fluid-soaked paper burst into flames.

There was something cathartic about watching things burn. Not that I was an arsonist, but these papers, these things my mother insisted on hoarding, had destroyed our normal lives. Now I spent most of my time hiding the truth or telling lies to cover things up. Burning these magazines and papers to ash felt like retribution.

Not that I liked to admit it, but more than one night I'd fantasized about burning the entire house down. I'd make sure my parents weren't inside, of course, but if the house and all my mother's crazy garbage went up in flames, maybe we could start over somewhere else. Start over in a nice, clean house where we weren't drowning in Rubbermaid containers and my mom's insanity.

Chapter Nine

NINA

After I finished my English homework, I took Gidget out in the backyard to play Frisbee. One of the strange features of our rental house, along with the shared driveway, was the fence that ran around our backyard also ran around West's. It made me wonder if whoever built these houses was from some strange cult trying to form their own compound. But that's probably also why the rent was cheaper than average, which, according to my mom, had been a major selling point.

And we'd needed a fenced backyard for Gidget, but this all-encompassing fence arrangement meant I had to try to teach her to stay in our allotted area. I had a feeling West's dad wouldn't be too happy to find a present from Gidget on his side of the property.

I threw the Frisbee toward West's house and Gidget ran full tilt, leaping into the air to catch it in her mouth. Then she trotted back to me and dropped it at my feet, exuding pure joy. That was one of the things I loved about her. She was always so happy in the moment, like life was meant to be lived to the fullest. Sometimes, I wish I could be more like her.

I kept an eye on West's house, watching for any movement. The entire house was wrapped up tight. I couldn't even see any light in the windows. What was that about? Did they have blackout curtains? Sometimes when the sun hit the glass just right, it looked like something was pushing the curtains against the glass, but that couldn't be right. No one put furniture in front of windows. That would be crazy.

I threw the Frisbee and it went wide, veering over behind West's shed. Gidget didn't seem to care that she'd be trespassing and ran over to where the Frisbee had flown. I followed along, just in case West's crabby dad was in the vicinity. I didn't want him yelling at her when my Frisbee skills were to blame.

Instead of grabbing the Frisbee and running back to our yard, Gidget sniffed the air like she'd caught scent of something and kept on going.

"Gidget, get back here." I ran after her and came upon a strange scene. West was sitting in a lawn chair on a basketball court overgrown with weeds, and he was barbecuing. The way he stood and glared at Gidget and me made me think we'd interrupted some type of strange man-ritual.

"What are you doing out here?" West demanded.

"Sorry, I didn't mean to intrude into your…" I waved my hand around to take in the weird area, "whatever this place is. My Frisbee throw was off, and Gidget must've caught scent of whatever you were barbecuing and came to investigate." I looked at the grill. He had a ton of paper in there and a few pieces of charcoal. Weird. The meat must still be in the cooler, because he wasn't cooking anything yet. "Are you sure that's how you're supposed to barbecue?" I asked.

"I'm sure it's none of your business."

I backed up a step. "Okay, Mr. Crabby Pants. Message received. Sorry I intruded on your sacred barbecue court."

He glared at me, so I patted Gidget on the head. "Come on, girl. Let's go home."

. . .

I went inside and checked on the taco meat my mom had put in the Crock Pot. The spicy aroma made my stomach rumble. I cut up some lettuce and tomatoes. By the time she came home with the shells, everything was ready. As we fixed our plates, I told her about West's strange behavior.

"Maybe that's his secret clubhouse out there," she said. "And girls aren't allowed."

"He's a little old for that," I said. "Maybe it's just a place where he can get away from his mom and dad."

My mom set her taco down. "That's sad."

"That entire house is sad. Did you ever notice that there aren't any lights on inside?" I took a bite of my taco. A few shreds of lettuce landed on my plate. I chewed and swallowed while I thought about this situation. "It's almost like they're trying to keep some secret locked up inside. It's kind of twisted. Like what if West's dad keeps his mom locked up in the basement?"

"I think you've watched too many creepy movies. The man might have antisocial issues, but I doubt he keeps his wife on lockdown." My mom frowned. "I wish we could do something to help."

A knock sounded on the back patio door. I went to investigate. West stood there with his hands shoved in his jeans pockets.

I slid the door open. "Hey, West. We're having tacos, if you want to join us."

He blinked at me like I was crazy. "Why do you keep

trying to feed me?"

I shrugged. "Just being neighborly." Plus as annoying as he could be, I doubted anyone took care of him. His dad didn't seem like the caregiving type.

"Listen, I didn't mean to yell at you earlier," he said. "You caught me off guard. I go out there to think."

"And barbecue?"

"Sometimes," he said. "Sometimes, like tonight, I just want to build a fire."

"They make these fabulous things called fire pits," I said.

The way his eyebrows slammed together told me he didn't think my comment was funny. And he had come over to make amends.

"Sorry. Sarcasm is my first language. It's cool that you go out there to think. And I'll do my best to stay away and keep Gidget in our yard."

The sound of his dad's giant SUV pulling up the driveway reverberated through the air.

"I should go." He ran back toward the basketball court.

Did he not want his dad to see us talking? That was weird. Then again, nothing about his family was normal.

Chapter Ten

I headed back to my barbecue court, which was a funny and accurate name. I checked to make sure the fire had burned to ash and then headed back to the house.

A house that always stunk of dust and decay, rather than Mexican food, which kind of made me mad. Why couldn't my parents pull their shit together? I opened the back door and smelled pizza.

My dad glanced up. "There you are. Come eat while the pizza is still warm."

And now I felt like a jerk for my earlier thoughts. My dad was probably doing the best he could. "Thanks. That smells great."

After dinner, I felt antsy. I pulled up the latest science fiction book I'd been reading, but it didn't hold my interest. My mind kept wandering to Nina. Oddly confrontational, yet attractive, Nina. What was her story?

I'd heard that they'd moved here when her parents

divorced. Her mom seemed normal, which made me wonder what her dad had done. Nina's pathological insistence on telling the truth made me think her dad must have lied or cheated.

Not that it was any of my business, but I liked to figure out why people behaved the way they did. I'd Googled a bunch of stuff about mental illness, hoping to find something to help my mom. All it had done was make me question my own sanity. Everyone was weird in one way or another. Most people figured out an acceptable way to behave while they were out in public.

My biggest fear was that one day I'd end up like my mom, trapped in my own house, drowning in useless possessions. This line of thought was getting me nowhere, so I changed into track pants and a sweatshirt and headed out for a run.

As my feet pounded the pavement, a wave of calmness flowed over me. This was why I ran. As I ran past the houses in the neighborhood, I noticed who had lights on and whose houses were dark like mine. Was no one home in the dark houses, or were other people drowning in junk like my mom?

• • •

The next day in social studies, Mr. Grant gave us a list of projects around town that needed volunteers. "I don't expect you to be altruistic at this age, so anyone who helps out with these projects will receive extra credit."

"Why?" a girl in the front row asked.

"Because people coming together to make their community a better place is important. Too many times people lose themselves in their own concerns or in online communities, and they forget to look around and take an interest in their neighbors' lives."

Charlie leaned over and said, "You don't have that

problem."

I snorted.

"Something you wanted to add, West?"

Busted. And for that, Charlie would pay...later. For now, I scanned the paper Mr. Grant had passed out. "What's going on with the library?"

"The Hilmer Library was built in 1912. It's suffered water damage from leaking pipes, and the heat and air need to be updated. It's become too expensive to maintain. Plans to build the new library have been delayed due to political red tape and funding. I believe they are supposed to break ground for the new building next spring. Brandt Recycling purchased the Hilmer building with the intention of turning it into a recycling center. There's some shelving and woodwork that can be salvaged before the conversion. Is that a project you'd be interested in working on?"

Not really, but I could fake it. "Sounds interesting."

"I suggest you gather a group of friends. I'll talk to the contractors and let you know when you can help."

The bell rang, saving me from further suck-uppery. Once we were in the hall, I punched Charlie. "Tell Matt it's your fault that he's been volunteered for salvage duty."

At lunch, I shared the good news with Matt. In his typical easygoing style, he shrugged. "Sure. Maybe they'll have something in there we can use at the nursery."

Matt and Charlie's dad owned Patterson Landscaping. Funny how they would inherit a thriving business, and I was going to inherit a house full of Rubbermaid boxes full of worthless junk.

It's not like you could choose who your parents were. I'd never understood how my antisocial dad could be their dad's brother. It's not like my uncle was everybody's friend; I knew he preferred to work outside with plants and trees rather than dealing with people, but at least he was able to interact with people and keep a business afloat.

When my mom first became ill, I'd spent a lot of time over at my cousins', hanging out with Matt and Charlie and Haley. I'd thought my mom was going through a phase, like when she'd bought a bunch of rusty, old farm tools at garage sales and put them up on shelves all over the kitchen, or when she'd made dozens of candles in old teacups. Instead of getting better, her collecting turned into hoarding. It was like someone had flipped a switch in her brain that made every item seem like a precious treasure she couldn't live without.

My dad dealt with all of it by storing her crap in Rubbermaid boxes. All I could do back then, and now, was sit back and watch as waves of boxes took over our house. Sneaking out what I could, when I could, felt like a small victory. I no longer dreamed of moving in with my cousins. I dreamed of graduating, moving out, and never looking back.

Chapter Eleven

NINA

Wednesday after school, I drove to the Hilmer Library. I parked in the side lot and walked around to the front entrance. Eager to get my book fix on, I jogged up the front steps, entered the building, and inhaled. *Ick*. Something wasn't right. Normally, the library had that magical book smell that reminded me of vanilla wafer cookies. Today, it smelled like wet towels that had been left in the hamper too long.

The librarian sat at her desk counting the coins from the HELP REHAB THE HILMER LIBRARY jar.

"How's it going?" I asked.

"Every penny helps," she said. "But I'm not sure how much longer we're going to be able to stay open."

"What? Why?" I knew the building was old and needed a lot of updating, but it had beautiful oak wainscoting running the length of the walls and amazing woodwork around the doors.

"A little girl went to get a drink from the water fountain

in the Children's section, and nothing came out because all the water that should have been going to the fountain has been seeping into the floorboards and the wall instead."

That explained the yucky smell. "Can someone fix it?"

"The guy who came to look at it just turned off the water line and suggested we wait for the wall and floor to dry out." She inhaled and then wrinkled her nose. "You can smell how well that's working."

"That stinks. Literally." I frowned. "Why isn't someone fixing the problem instead of hoping it goes away?"

She sighed and started sliding pennies into a brown paper wrapper. "Every time something around here breaks, which seems to be way too often, the city says it makes more sense to put the money toward the new library they plan to build next spring."

"In theory, that makes sense, but what are you supposed to do in the meantime?" I asked.

"We're putting together a group of people to try to raise funds to fix this place up and keep it open until the new library is built." She pointed to a library table stacked high with books. "In the meantime, we're hedging our bets by selling off books for a dollar a piece. If we do have to shut down, there won't be as much to pack."

Since it was for a good cause, I bought half a dozen books.

Later that night, I sat reading on the couch, when Gidget came over to join me. And by join me, I mean she wedged her long, skinny nose under my book and pushed it up so she could play the world's largest lap puppy.

"Gidget." I set my book down and looked into her soulful brown eyes. "Are you not getting the attention you deserve?"

She made a sound that my mom and I described as her complaining yodel. "What's that about?" I asked as I ran my hand over her silky blonde head. She yodeled louder.

My mom walked into the living room. "She is trying to

tell you we're out of chewies."

"Oh, no." I hugged Gidget. "The horror."

She whined like she agreed with me. "It's okay, girl. I can run to the store."

"It's not like she can't wait until tomorrow," my mom said.

"No big deal. I need gas anyway." I slid out from under Gidget and looked at my fur-covered jeans and shirt. "The good thing about running to the pet store is no one cares if you're covered in fur."

West's dad had parked his ridiculously large SUV further up the driveway. Backing out next to his car was almost impossible. Thank goodness I only had to back up next to West's Ford Fusion, which wasn't a big deal.

I set my phone on the dash and checked my mirror before backing up slowly. My cell buzzed, and I turned my head to see who the text was from. The scraping crunch of metal on metal set my teeth on edge. I stomped on the brake and stared at my hands where I'd turned the wheel the slightest bit to the right when I'd checked the text. Son of a... A cold sweat beaded my forehead as I pulled forward and parked. It took me a moment to unclench my hands from the steering wheel. Maybe it wasn't that bad.

No one had come running, so the crash hadn't been that loud, which gave me hope. Less sound had to mean less damage. Right? Hands shaking, I undid my seat belt and climbed out to assess the carnage.

My Jeep sat up higher than West's car, so I'd scraped a foot of his paint and ripped off his passenger-side mirror. It lay on the ground, mostly in one piece. Maybe I could stick it back on like a Lego. Would it snap back into place?

I picked up the mirror and held it up to its former position. Nope. It was broken clean off. Acid surged in my stomach. Now what? Shit. I was going to have to confess. And since I couldn't knock on his door, I was going to have to call him.

Damn. Damn. Damn. It's okay. I can do this. Not a big deal. Right... I dialed his number.

"Nina?" He sounded surprised to hear from me.

"Hey, West. I wanted to let you know...we can drive to school whatever time you want tomorrow."

"What are you talking about? Why would we ride together?"

"Well, the damage isn't bad," I said, stalling for time. "It's your passenger-side mirror, really, or lack of one."

"What in the hell are you— Oh my God...did you hit my car?"

"Yes."

I could hear the sound of him moving, and then the front door flew open. He stalked down the driveway.

"I'm sorry." I held the mirror out to him.

He snatched it from my hands and stared at it like he couldn't believe what he was holding. "You hit my car."

"I did." This was when me not lying really sucked.

He walked over to his car and ran his hand down the area where the paint was scratched, and then he inspected where the mirror used to be. I bit back a nervous laugh when he tried pressing it back against the car the same way I had.

"We could try some glue, or maybe duct tape," I offered.

"Duct tape?" He practically spit the words out at me. "You want to duct tape my mirror back on my car?"

"Not the best idea, I know. I'm sure my insurance will pay for it." I hoped. I dialed my mom. "Can you come outside? I kind of hit West's car and ripped his mirror off."

"Oh, no." She literally ran outside and joined us.

West held the mirror out to her like he was offended by it.

"Okay." My mom took the mirror from him. "It's a pretty clean break. I have some Gorilla Glue in the house."

"You're not *gluing* my mirror back on," West stated.

"I suggested duct tape," I told my mom.

"What's going on out here?" West's dad came out the front door, slamming it behind him.

West's dad was not going to yell at him for something I'd done. "I'm sorry. It was my fault. I clipped West's mirror."

His dad focused on me, and suddenly I doubted the wisdom of using myself as a human shield. The man was large and scary.

"We have insurance," my mom piped up as she dialed someone on her phone. "And Nina will be happy to give West a ride to school until his car is fixed. They're going to the same place, after all." She spoke to someone, telling him or her about the accident. "Just give me a moment to explain." She walked a few feet into the yard, talking fast. A moment later she came back. "I reported it. You can get a quote and my insurance will take care of it. There's no need to freak out, Mr. Smith."

This news didn't seem to comfort West's dad. He stood there with his face so red it looked like steam should be shooting out of his ears. "I warned you when you signed the rental agreement that you needed to be careful about the driveway."

"It was an accident." I enunciated each syllable like that might make him better understand the term.

"Any more accidents like this, and you'll have to find another place to live."

"We're sorry," my mom said. "And it won't happen again. West, why don't you come over to our house so you and Nina can talk about what time you want to go to school tomorrow. And your father can get back to whatever it was he was doing."

West froze like he wasn't sure what he was supposed to do.

I reached for his arm. "Come on. This will only take a

minute."

West allowed me to pull him toward my house. His father stomped off in the opposite direction.

Once we were inside, my mom said, "Honey, why don't you two come sit at the kitchen table, and I'll pour us all some hot tea."

"I don't want tea," West said. "I want my car in one piece."

"We'll get your car fixed." I stood and went to the cabinet over the microwave where we kept the chocolate stash. I grabbed a handful of Hershey kisses and brought them back to the table. "Have some chocolate. It will make you feel better."

"No, it won't." He stood. "Be ready to drive to school at a quarter after seven tomorrow."

"What? Why?" Was he insane? I didn't leave until seven forty-five. "We don't have to be in homeroom until eight fifteen."

"I like to go early, and you ripped my mirror off, so that's when we're going."

I pulled my keys from my pocket. "Here. Just take my Jeep. I'll have Lisa pick me up at a normal time."

West reached for the keys.

"Sorry, we can't do that," my mom said. "Our insurance wouldn't cover him."

Crap. Maybe I could bargain with him. "Seven thirty?"

"Seven twenty-five," he said.

Great.

About half an hour after West left, Jason came in the front door. He looked at my mom and then at me. "What happened?"

"I hit West's car and ripped his mirror off."

"Nice," he said.

"Way to be supportive." And that gave me an idea. "You could help me out by giving West a ride to school."

"Sorry. I can't be late to my co-op."

Damn. I'd forgotten about that.

. . .

It wasn't until I woke up the next morning that I realized I'd also forgotten to set my alarm for an earlier time. I had twenty minutes until West expected me to be in the driveway. While I wasn't high maintenance, it took at least that long for my hair to dry. I took the fastest shower of my life and blew as much wetness from my hair as I could before giving up and wrangling it into a braid. Then I threw on a pair of jeans, one of my favorite Harry Potter turtle necks, and my Converse. A quick swipe of mascara made it look like I might be awake and ready to start my day, which totally wasn't true. Behold the magic of eye makeup.

By some sort of miracle, I was only five minutes late. West stood leaning against my Jeep staring at his cell.

"Sorry, I forgot to change the time on my alarm clock."

Rather than respond, he continued to stare at his phone. "West?"

"Hold on," he muttered.

I watched the time on my cell change from seven thirty to seven thirty-three before he looked up. "I had to finish that chapter. I'm sure you understand."

I nodded. "I do." At least he wasn't griping at me. I climbed in and unlocked the passenger door so he could join me. Then I started the Jeep and backed out at a snail's pace, making sure not to do any further damage to his car. "Shared driveways are a stupid idea."

"You won't get any argument from me, and I'm sure that disappoints you," he said. "Do you know why we have a shared driveway?"

"Because fate knew we were destined to go to the Valentine's Dance and fall madly in love?" I said, just to mess with him.

He glanced sideways at me, like he wasn't sure if I was serious or not.

"Relax. I'm joking."

"Good. Because I don't believe in all that fate and destiny crap."

I noticed he didn't argue the going-to-the-dance part, which was interesting. "You don't believe in fate?"

Chapter Twelve

"No." Maybe I had before my mom's mental illness took over our lives, but now I couldn't see how fate or destiny thought my family deserved this mess.

"Why not?" she asked.

Time to turn this back on her. "Because things just happen. There isn't always some cosmic reason."

"I read somewhere that life is a series of twists and turns you don't see coming, but they end up leading you where you belong."

"Really? So you knocking the mirror off my car is part of some grand design? I don't buy it."

"Maybe," she said. "Or maybe fate wanted us to spend some quality time together so I can help you see that the world is a brighter place than you think it is."

I snorted. "The world will be a brighter place once I have a scholarship that lets me move far away." Wait. Why had I shared that? Maybe because even with her crazy beliefs and bad driving skills she was easy to talk to.

"What scholarships are you applying for?" she asked, like she was actually interested.

"I'm hoping for one of the Merit scholarships. With my grades I should have a decent chance."

"I applied for a few of those, too. Although I'm not sure I have faith in the system. A lot of people apply."

"That's oddly cynical. Why go through the trouble of writing the essays and filling out the forms if you don't think you'll get one?"

"My mom wanted me to apply. There's a chance I could get one. If I don't, she said it's good practice for when things don't go your way in life. One of those life-lesson scenarios."

"Have you ever noticed that those always suck? No one ever calls a happy event a life lesson."

She laughed. "I never thought of it that way, but you're right. Maybe life lesson is the grown-up code for things that suck. Even if I do get a scholarship, I have no idea what I want to major in or even what college I should go to. How about you?"

"I've been accepted to a few of my first-choice schools and a few I'm not sure about. As far as a job, goes, I know I want to do something that lets me travel. I don't want to be tied down to one place. I like math, so maybe something in accounting or engineering."

"Those aren't people person jobs, and you seem like a people person."

"I do?" *Why does she think that?* "Because most of the time, people annoy the crap out of me."

She laughed. "I'm pretty sure that is one of those things you aren't supposed to say out loud."

That didn't meld with what she'd said before. "I thought you were the honesty-is-the-best-policy person."

"Lying is wrong, but sometimes people share things they

shouldn't." Her expression darkened.

"Like what?"

"Nothing," she said. "It's stupid."

"We're stuck together for at least ten more minutes. So you might as well spill it."

She stopped at a red light and picked at the hem on her right sleeve, pulling a loose thread and then yanking if off. "Well…when my dad broke things off with us, he should have kept the details of his other life to himself. I think he felt the need to confess, which just made the situation worse. He could have said he met someone else. We didn't need all the gory details. I read somewhere that you have to carry your own water, meaning it's crappy to confess to make yourself feel better, if it will make the person hearing the confession feel worse."

The light turned green and we moved with the flow of traffic. How should I respond to her sharing something so personal? This level of honesty was foreign to me. "My family goes with the ostrich approach. Stick your head in the ground, ignore the problem, and hope it goes away."

"You mean like your mom being sick?"

I nodded. "My dad likes to pretend everything is fine."

"And your mom?" Nina asked.

It felt like I was jogging through a minefield. "I think… that she's been this way for so long…she's forgotten what life was like before."

"If we weren't on the road, I'd be hugging you right now," Nina said, with a catch in her voice. "Because that is one of the saddest things I've ever heard."

It was one of the most honest things I'd ever said. It made a spot in my chest ache. Words poured out of my mouth before I could stop them. "It's such a cop-out, both she and my dad. If she acts like it's normal, then she doesn't have to admit it's a problem. If my dad acts like it's all okay, then he doesn't have to try to convince her to find treatment."

"Are there other doctors she could see? Maybe get a second opinion?"

"I've asked that same question over and over again, and neither of my parents are willing to try anything new."

"That's so frustrating and just plain wrong."

Not like I was going to argue with her.

"I've been racking my brain about something that might be nice for your mom," Nina said. "Do you think she'd want to listen to some audiobooks? You can buy them and download them onto your phone or tablet."

That was actually a good thought. "I'll mention it to her."

. . .

While I sat in homeroom, I thought about how different Nina was from Vicky. Nina actually seemed to be concerned for my family. I'd given Vicky the same story about my mom being ill, but she never offered any suggestions about how she might be able to help. I'd never expected her to. Then Nina comes along with her weird hugging family who likes to feed everyone...which was actually kind of nice. Maybe I could tell her what was really going on with my mom. It would be such a relief not to have to keep so much of my life secret from the girl I liked.

Whoa. Where did that come from? Unless I could argue my way out of it, I was stuck taking Nina to the dance, but nothing would happen after that. Right? Nina could be a friend. And that would be okay because, despite what I'd said to Vicky, my only two friends were Matt and Charlie. If Nina proved trustworthy, maybe I could add her to that small select group.

Chapter Thirteen

Driving West to school this morning had proved enlightening. His family was one messed-up household. Not that my family with my lying, cheating, polygamist father was the standard for normal, but still. Why wouldn't his dad seek a second opinion for his mom? Why would his mom pretend everything was okay? How sick was she? Was she dying? Good God, how did they even deal with something like that, if she was?

I was glad West had liked my audiobook idea. It made me feel like I was helping a little bit. And from what I'd seen, he needed someone to help him out every once in a while. The image of him sitting alone on the overgrown basketball court burning papers in the barbecue pit was something that would stick in my head forever, filed under Sad and Strange Male Behavior.

There was probably a whole lot of guy behavior I'd never understand, but maybe I could help West, if he'd let me. I could make a gift box containing graham crackers, marshmallows, and chocolate bars and set it out on one of the lawn chairs. That way, when he was out there engaging in his manly, brooding alone time, he'd have the world's best snack. I had noticed that there were two lawn chairs, which made me wonder if anyone else ever sat out there with him. His dad mustn't know what he was doing, which was probably the reason he had freaked out when Gidget and I interrupted him.

By lunchtime, I decided the s'mores plan might be a waste of good chocolate because I wasn't sure if West would appreciate my actions or be annoyed by them. He seemed to run hot and cold.

Lisa and I sat at our normal table in the cafeteria. West didn't join us today. Not that he needed to, because we weren't dating.

"Who's he sitting with?" Lisa asked.

I glanced over to where West sat. "I think those guys are fraternal twins, Matt and Charlie something?"

"Their family owns that landscaping business," Lisa said. "What is it…Peterson…no…Patterson…that's their last name."

"Right. They're both kind of cute. I could ask West if either of them are seeing anyone."

"No thank you. I'm enjoying a drama-free life right now."

"You sound like Jason." Which gave me a funny idea. "Maybe that's the universe's plan," I teased. "To fix you up with my brother."

Lisa laughed. "I don't think so. Your brother flees the room whenever I come over."

"He does?" I hadn't noticed.

Lisa nodded. "Ever since I walked in when he was peeing, he hasn't been able to speak to me. I assured him I didn't see anything, but I think it traumatized him."

"Please, up until a few years ago, he used to pee outside on the bushes."

"*Ewwww.*" Lisa wrinkled her nose. "That's just wrong."

"I'm pretty sure my dad taught him to do that. I think it's a guy thing." The memory made me equal parts sad and mad. When my dad was home he'd seemed happy, not like a guy who needed another family because we weren't enough. "I'm going to end up in therapy one day because of him."

"Hey," Lisa broke her Twinkie in half and passed me a piece. "Childhood trauma is what makes you a stronger person. If everyone had the ideal life, my mom wouldn't have a job."

Lisa's mom was a family counselor. When we'd first moved here, my mom had dragged my brother and me to counseling. I'd scoffed at the idea, but it had ended up being a good thing. One day, Lisa had been there waiting for a ride home. We'd talked and bonded over our love of books.

"Does your mom ever get tired of listening to other people's problems?" I asked. It didn't seem like a fun way to spend your day.

Lisa shrugged. "Your mom tries to hug everyone or feed them. My mom tries to talk them through their issues. Same thing, different delivery method."

• • •

When I went to meet West at my Jeep after school, he wasn't there. Since he liked to be everywhere early, I figured he must have stayed after class to talk to someone. No big deal. It was a sunny fifty degrees, and being outside after being trapped in classrooms all day felt good. I leaned against my bumper, pulled out my phone, clicked on the Kindle app, and lost myself in a story about shape-shifting dragons.

People shuffled past me, and cars pulled out of the lot. Haze from the gravel dust drifted through the air and landed on my screen. I wiped my phone with my shirt. A thread poked out from the end of my sleeve. I wrapped it around my index finger twice and then tugged, breaking it off.

"Why did you do that?" West asked.

I glanced up. He approached with a frown on his face.

"Why did I do what?"

"Pull out the thread on your sleeve." He grabbed my hand and turned it palm up, pointing at the shirt cuff, which looked off kilter. "You pulled the thread and now it's uneven."

West held my hand in a familiar way and didn't seem to think anything about it. I'd hugged him once before, but this skin-to-skin contact caused butterflies to flit around in my stomach.

"I guess you're right," I said. "But stray threads make me crazy."

"It would be a shame to ruin this," he narrowed his eyes at my shirt. "Are those snitches on your shirt?"

"Yes. Snitches and brooms. But you only notice if you stare; otherwise, it looks like a pattern."

"You're one of those people who dreams about going to Hogwarts, aren't you?"

"Do you mean the real Hogwarts or the amusement park, because the answer to both is yes."

"I'm sure your owl was blown off course in a storm." He released my hand. "Do you mind if we run an errand on the way home? My dad wants me to pick something up from the hardware store."

"If I said it wasn't okay, would you change your plans?" I asked, just to be contrary.

"Do you have somewhere you need to be?" he asked.

"No. People say, 'If that's okay with you' all the time. Rarely does anyone say, 'No, that's not okay.' So I was just messing with you because I wanted to see how you'd react. You know, testing the balance of the universe and all that."

West shook his head, but he was smiling while he did it. A smile that made my heart rate kick up a notch.

"Get in the Jeep, Luna," he said.

Chapter Fourteen

Nina backed out of the parking spot and put the Jeep in drive. We exited the gravel lot and took a right onto the main road. I glanced at her shirt. "How much *Harry Potter* memorabilia do you own?" I'd read the series multiple times, but stopped short of buying fan merchandise.

"I don't know you well enough to share that information," she said, "because I'm pretty sure you'd mock me."

I probably would. "Let's start with the basics. I'm going to guess you own the hardback books, the paperbacks, and the ebooks."

"Of course I do. The hardbacks live on my bookshelf in a place of honor, I carry the paperbacks around with me when I want to read them, and I have them on my phone in case of emergencies."

"Interesting logic," I said. "What qualifies as a *Harry Potter* ebook emergency?"

"Being stuck in line or in traffic or in a really boring

lecture at school."

"You read during class?" I hadn't thought she'd break the rules like that. It made her more interesting.

"Yep. I'm a rebel."

"A hugging, hippie-chick, bookworm kind of rebel?" I asked.

"I'm not one for labels, but that works."

She grinned at me, and the weight I perpetually carried around on my shoulders seemed to lighten.

"So what are we buying at the hardware store?" she asked.

And the weight came crashing back down. "My dad asked me to pick up some storage boxes."

"Let me guess, just like the driveway, he likes everything stored in its prescribed spot."

The absurdity of her statement made me laugh. Sure my dad liked everything neat and tidy. An impossible feat with years worth of junk mail, old magazines, newspapers, the cardboard tubes left over from paper towels, and God-knew-what-else, filling up our house.

"Are you okay?" Nina asked as she turned into the hardware store lot and parked. "Because that wasn't a happy laugh."

And this was exactly why I shouldn't make new friends or, apparently, talk to anyone. The fact that she actually seemed to care and wanted to help had me spilling my guts. "It's a constant balancing act at my house. My dad wants everything a certain way, and my mom wants the opposite. I try to make both of them happy, but sometimes it's impossible."

"I'm sorry."

I nodded, afraid if I opened my mouth I'd confess everything...how my entire life was an elaborate web of lies.

Nina undid her seat belt and scooted closer. "You need a hug."

I didn't make a smart-ass comment or push her away. Instead, I met her halfway and let her put her arms around me. It was awkward since we were in a Jeep but, by coincidence, our faces lined up perfectly. I stared into her eyes for a moment seeing nothing but concern and kindness. I closed my eyes and leaned my forehead against hers. She smelled good…sort of sweet, but not flowery. I inhaled. "What is that smell?" I asked.

"Apple mint shampoo," she said. "It's a happy smell."

"I like it." I opened my eyes. "And I think I like you, too."

She grinned. "You're not so bad yourself."

"And I've read *Harry Potter*," I said, like I was arguing my case.

She glanced at my mouth. I took that as my cue and leaned in. Time seemed to slow down as she leaned in to meet me halfway.

Chapter Fifteen

NINA

Holy crap. West was going to kiss me. I leaned in and––

Honk honk!

I jerked away from him and glanced around.

"I don't think they were honking at us," I said, which was probably one of the stupidest statements known to man. Ugh. Why had I said that?

"We should probably go inside," he said.

And the moment was gone. "Right."

We headed into the store while I mentally cursed whoever had interrupted what could have been an amazing first kiss. Was West thinking about our missed opportunity too? If he was, he didn't show it. Walking at an easy pace, like he didn't have a care or a frustration in the world, he headed to the area with all the organizational and storage items.

We were halfway down the aisle when I saw the holy grail. It was one of those floor-to-ceiling bookshelves, the kind you hook together to make an entire wall devoted to books. I ran my fingertips reverently over the box. "I want one."

West looked at the label. "You dream about having an entire room full of floor-to-ceiling bookshelves with one of those library ladders, don't you?"

"Of course," I said. "Doesn't everyone?"

"If there was an end-of-the-world apocalypse and you had to pick a store to live in, which one would you choose?"

Interesting question. "My first thought is the library, but they wouldn't have enough food. So I'm thinking a bookstore with an attached restaurant or cafe."

"I'd pick a Sam's Club. Tons of food and a decent selection of books." He walked over to a stack of tubs and grabbed four of them, adding the lids to the top box.

"What is your dad going to do with those? I asked.

"He'll organize something, and that will make him feel better." He shrugged. "I don't get it, but when he's happy, my life is easier."

I glanced back at the floor-to-ceiling bookshelf. I didn't have enough space for something like that in my room, but I could use a smaller one. "I want to look at the bookshelves for a minute." There was a four-foot shelf that looked far more manageable. Since the box it came in was only a foot wide, it had to be the kind of furniture that needed to be assembled. "This one might work."

"Have you ever put furniture like that together?" he asked. "Because there are always pieces left over, and it never looks like the picture on the box."

"I helped my mom put our coffee table together, but it was pretty simple. Just the top and the legs." I tried to move the box so I could see the directions. It didn't budge. "How can a box this small be so heavy?"

"Maybe the universe is trying to tell you that's not the bookshelf for you," West teased.

"Very funny, but you might be right. I'd rather buy one

that doesn't need to be assembled."

"That's a much better plan."

We paid for West's storage boxes and then I drove him home, which was my home, too, which was weird. "You never told me why our houses share a driveway and a backyard."

"Identical twins built the houses, and it was stated in their wills that the houses had to be sold together for the remaining relatives to receive any money from the sale. Otherwise, it would all go to charity. The will also stipulated the buyer, my dad, would pay a reduced price on the property if he promised not to sell whichever house he didn't live in, but he was allowed to rent it."

"So the twins were so close they shared a backyard and a driveway?" That seemed like overkill.

"They probably didn't mind, plus I bet it was cheaper than pouring two driveways and it took less fencing."

As I pulled into the driveway, I looked at the houses with new eyes. "That's so weird. I never realized the houses were the same on the outside." Structurally, the front doors and the windows were in the same place. Mine had cream-colored siding, gray shutters, and a gray front door. West's was the mirror image with gray siding and cream-colored shutters and front door. It was sort of creepy.

"I helped my dad paint after the last renters left, so I've seen your whole house. They're the same on the outside, but the insides are completely different."

Why did he sound sad about that? The conversation was lagging, but I wasn't sure what I was supposed to do. Was a good-bye kiss on the horizon? Stalling for time, I said, "This is totally me being nosy, but why were you late meeting me after school?"

"I had to check in with Mr. Grant about an extra-credit project for social studies. If we do something good for the community, like have a fundraiser, or help clean up a park, and then write a report about it, we get extra credit."

"That's cool," I said. "yet slightly manipulative. What's your project?"

"I'm thinking about working on the Hilmer building."

"The old library they're trying to keep open?" As if he wasn't perfect enough, now he was saving libraries. I almost swooned.

He sat back and gave me an odd look. "I don't think anyone is trying to keep it open. They're asking for volunteers to salvage what they can before they turn it into a recycling center."

Abort swoon and report to battle stations. "That can't be right. There's a group of people trying to raise funds to keep it open until the new library is completed."

"I hate to rain on your idealistic parade, but Mr. Grant said the company who bought it has already scheduled the rehab to convert it to a warehouse for a recycling center. It's a done deal."

"They can't take away the town's library. I know there are some issues, but the woodwork is beautiful."

"Have you been there lately?' West asked. "The place smells like mildew."

Okay, the place did smell a little funny, but I wasn't about to admit that. Besides, a little funding for repairs and a good cleaning with bleach should take care of any problems. I had to make him see reason. "Haven't you watched those shows on HGTV where they restore old houses?"

"Not on my top-ten list of shows to watch," West said. "Besides, I'm not the one who told them to convert the building to a recycling center; I just volunteered to help for extra credit. And they're going to build another library."

"Yes, but it's not completed yet. And you're volunteering to do something anti-book. How can you do that?"

"Anti-book? That's ridiculous. It's not like I'm setting

books on fire."

"I understand that, but overall you're wrong. I'd love to stay and argue, but I need to let Gidget outside before she makes a puddle that I will have to clean up. For now, we'll have to agree to disagree and continue this later." I climbed out and jogged up to my front door.

I let myself into the house and Gidget wiggle-walked up to greet me. "Who's a good dog?" I reached down and rubbed both of her ears at the same time. She closed her eyes and gave a canine snuffle of joy. And that's why dogs were so awesome. They were an attitude adjustment in furry form. I set my bag down and hugged her, letting my irritation drift away. She ran to the back door and I let her out.

What had I expected from West, anyway? It's not like he and I were destined to be soul mates and agree on all topics. That would probably be boring. West was just a cute guy with great hair and amazing eyes who lived next door. A guy who smelled fabulous and whose smile made my heart beat a little faster. A guy who'd almost kissed me half an hour ago until that stupid car honked at us. He was also a guy who seemed to have inherited his father's neat-freak tendencies because he liked pointing out when things were dusty, or could possibly harbor mold or mildew. That wasn't normal teen guy behavior.

I grabbed my cell and called Lisa to catch her up on the latest not-not-my-boyfriend saga.

"My first response is, oh my God, he tried to kiss you. My second response is, how could he volunteer to turn that amazing old building into some sort of recycling center?"

"I know, right? This leaves me only one choice."

"Argue with him until he caves?"

"How well you know me."

Chapter Sixteen

I was surprised Nina hadn't stayed to argue. Then again, my dad wouldn't be thrilled if Gidget peed on the floor, so it was good that she didn't always have to have the last word. And this was an argument she would most definitely lose.

Just because a building housed books didn't make it sacred, or some sort of shrine to literature. There was no reason to hold on to old things when there were plenty of new libraries and books in the world. Sure, people might have to drive a little farther to check out books, but it's not like there was a shortage. Besides, the company that purchased the building wanted to turn it into a recycling center. That was a good thing.

I may have fallen ass backward into this project because of Charlie, but it seemed like a karmic gift. I dreamt about renting a Dumpster and emptying all the dusty old crap out of my house. If I couldn't do it at home, at least I could help transform an old building into a place that would help keep things out of landfills.

I grabbed the boxes from the backseat and walked around to the patio doors because there was zero room to maneuver if I went in the front door. And I didn't want to die in a storage box landslide.

Funny how I'd panicked for a moment when we pulled in the driveway. Almost kissing Nina hadn't been something I'd planned. The desire to kiss her came out of nowhere. When she'd hugged me it was like everything had fallen into place— kind of like her whole universe theory, which made it funny and annoying at the same time.

I let myself in and the sight of my mom sitting at the kitchen table with two cups of coffee threw me off balance. She pushed the second cup toward the chair I normally sat in. "I was hoping you'd be home before the coffee went cold. Where were you?"

Accusation was clear in her voice, like I'd abandoned her. Maybe if she left the house every once in a while she would find some new people to talk to.

"I ran an errand after school." I sat and picked up the cup of coffee. It wasn't hot, but it was warm enough. "Thanks for the coffee."

"You're welcome. I thought about making PB&Js, but I wasn't sure if you were having dinner next door or not."

"Not tonight."

"You like her, don't you?" My mom smiled over the rim of her coffee cup.

"Nina? Yes and no."

"That's a strange answer," she said.

"It's been a strange day."

"Tell me about her. What does she like to do?" my mom asked.

"She likes books, Harry Potter, dogs, and moldy old buildings."

"Those are mostly good qualities." My mom ducked her head. "I have a confession."

Oh, hell. What did she do?

"I watch her family from my bedroom window."

"You do?" That was odd. "I didn't think you could get to your window." Most of the windows in our house were hidden behind walls of boxes.

"When they moved in, I was curious, so I shifted things around so I could watch them. It's more interesting than watching television."

"Instead of spying on Nina's family, you could go out and meet them, interact like you used to."

"I might like that one day." She sipped her coffee. "But I'd have to talk to your father first. He doesn't like me to leave the house."

"He doesn't?" Was this part of her mental illness, or did my dad actually discourage her from socializing? "It's nice outside. We could take our coffee on the back porch right now, if you want. No one else has to be involved."

She adjusted the front of her robe, pulling it tighter "I'm not dressed. Maybe tomorrow."

The small glimmer of hope that had been growing inside of me fizzled out. "Whenever you're ready." My stomach growled. Suddenly, it felt like I was starving. "What do you want for dinner?"

"Whatever you feel like cooking." She stood. "Why don't you call me when it's ready. I'll be in my room."

"Sure, Mom." She padded back down the hallway in her slippers. I closed my eyes and resisted the urge to lay my head on the table. For a few moments, I'd thought she might be getting better…that she was interested in the outside world again…that she might want to go outside and rejoin society or, at the very least, cook dinner, since she was supposed to be the one taking care of me. Sometimes I was amazed by my own stupidity. She wasn't getting better, and she probably never would. I pushed up from my chair, feeling like I had a hundred-pound weight balanced on my head.

I opened the refrigerator and grabbed a package of Ball Park franks. Gourmet it was not, but I was hungry. I zapped the hotdogs in the microwave and ate three of them before I put one on the table for my mom. My dad could make his own. I headed to my room, stopping for a moment outside of my mom's door to let her know food was on the table and I was going to do my homework.

Once I was in my room, I put my phone on the charger and pulled a book up on my tablet—the same book I'd been reading this morning when Nina had given me a ride to school. Would she still want to give me a ride to school tomorrow? Then again, it's not like she had a choice, since she was the reason my car was in the shop.

The next morning, I waited for her in the driveway, reading on my cell just like the day before. She appeared, on time, without saying a word. After she unlocked the doors and climbed in, I joined her. She didn't try to kick me out, so I guess we were good.

Chapter Seventeen

West read his book on the way to school. It was almost like yesterday never happened…like he'd never tried to kiss me. He had tried to kiss me, hadn't he? Of course he had. Why else would he lean in like that? And the look in his eyes when he'd done it, like he saw something he wanted…someone he wanted. My face flushed as I replayed the scene in my head. Was West thinking about the not-quite-a-kiss, too, or was he reading his book. After a few minutes of silence I caved.

"Are you not talking to me?"

"I was waiting and saving my energy for when you launched into a we-must-keep-the-moldy-old-library open debate," he said.

"I'm not typically a morning debater," I said.

"I didn't realize you had to schedule these things."

I laughed. "Catch me around lunch and I'll be ready to go."

"Or you could just have your opinion, and I could have

mine."

"Yes, but yours would still be wrong. Next topic. Have you heard back about your car?"

"Nice segue, and yes, it shouldn't take long to fix. They're waiting on a part."

"Good." I prayed it wouldn't be an expensive part. "I am really sorry about it."

"I know," he said. "It was a *stupid* mistake." He emphasized the word *stupid*, like he was baiting me.

Game on. "One you could just as easily have made," I said.

"But I didn't. And I thought you didn't like to debate in the morning."

"I might have changed my mind."

"Okay. Well there's no way for you to win the argument about hitting my car, so feel free to move on to the library." He cracked his knuckles and gave off an air of self-satisfaction.

"Smug much?" I asked.

"Only when it's called for."

Was it wrong that I was enjoying this? I cleared my throat like I was about to make an announcement. "First off, libraries are near and dear to my heart, so the idea of gutting one and turning it into a recycling center annoys me. I Googled it last night, and the nearest library is forty minutes away. So I'd like to file a complaint that the rehab date has been set when the new library hasn't even been built yet."

"And who would you like to file this complaint with? Because the last time I checked, that's not my department."

"Right now you are the sole representative of the anti-library coalition, so I'm filing the complaint with you."

"I refuse to accept it."

I laughed as I pulled into the parking lot. Once I found a spot and parked, I released my seat belt and turned to him. What would he do if I leaned in and kissed him? I could do it. Just lean toward him a little bit to see how he'd react…but what if he didn't notice or, worse yet, blew me off? For now, I'd stick with talking. "Eventually, you'll concede that I'm right and you're wrong." I grabbed my backpack and scooted out of the car. Before closing the door, I added, "And you're still taking me to the Valentine's Dance." Just for fun.

I headed toward the sidewalk, waiting to see how West would respond. He caught up and fell into step beside me. "Interesting debating style. Make a grand announcement and then flee. Does it normally work?"

I grinned. "I haven't tried it before, so I guess we'll have to wait and see."

"You're a fascinating girl, Nina. But I'm not taking you to the Valentine's Dance."

"Why not? What's your objection?"

"It's the principle," he said. "Dances are ridiculous."

I looked him up and down. "You can't dance."

"I can dance," he said. "I choose not to."

"Right." I was having so much fun joking with West, I didn't want to push my luck, so I let the subject drop for now.

For the rest of the week, I gave him a ride to school. We laughed and talked a lot, but he never tried to kiss me. I didn't get it. It's not like he was only hanging out with me because he was stuck with me. Right? I mean, sure we lived next door to each other, and I gave him a ride to school, and…I didn't like where this line of thinking was taking me.

Friday, on the way home from school, West said, "So what are you doing tonight?"

Oh my God. Was he finally asking me on a date? Lisa and I had our Friday night bookstore plans, and I'd never cancel on her just because a guy asked me out. Maybe he'd want to do something on Saturday. "Lisa and I are going to the bookstore tonight. What are your big plans for the weekend?"

"The most exciting part of my weekend will be getting

my car back, which means we won't have to ride to school together on Monday."

Oh. He didn't have to sound so thrilled about it. "That's cool."

"You won't have to wake up early," he said. "I thought that would make you happy."

"I hadn't thought about it like that," I said. "And I guess you can go back to arriving at school really early for no apparent reason."

And the conversation kind of stalled out. He looked at his cell, and I tried to come up with something to say that didn't make me sound desperate. When I parked, he didn't look up from his phone. He just said, "See you later." And he climbed out of the car.

Hmmm... I wish the conversation had ended on a more positive note. What's done was done. Disappointment and doubt lapped at the corners of my mind. I did my best to ignore them. When I entered the house, Gidget ran to greet me. I sat down and hugged her. Dogs were good. Boys were confusing. And dating/not dating, or whatever it was we'd been doing, sucked.

Chapter Eighteen

I picked up my car Saturday afternoon and drove around town just because I could. Having my car back felt like freedom. Sure, my dad would have let me borrow the Humvee if I asked, but I also would have received an unwanted lecture. Plus, the thing burned through gas like crazy.

My Fusion didn't go through a quarter of the gas his car did. And it looked a lot cooler doing it. I drove past restaurants that had hearts in their windows. Valentine's Day wasn't too far away. What was I going to do about Nina and the dance?

My cell rang and a call from Matt came through the speakers. "Hey, Matt. What's up?"

"We're out at Bixby's. Come meet us."

"Okay." The call disconnected. Why were they at Bixby's? The retro burger place wasn't one of our normal hangouts because it catered to families.

When I pulled into the parking lot, I was surprised to see it was crowded. The marquee announced they were showing classic movies on a newly installed eighty-inch flat-screen television. Whenever anyone said something was a classic, I always wondered who made that distinction. My dad watched *Jaws* any time it was on television. A crazy old guy took a scientist and a cop, who was afraid of the water, into the middle of the ocean to track down and kill a giant man-eating shark...with a rifle. I didn't get it.

I parked in the first open spot and then went to look for Matt and Charlie. They were seated inside at one of the chrome tables with black vinyl stools. I sat next to Matt and grabbed one of his fries. "What movie are they playing?"

"*Harry Potter*," Matt said, "and get your own food."

"Why do you want to watch *Harry Potter*?" Neither of them had read the books, and I was pretty sure they hadn't seen the movies.

"We're not here for the movie." Matt inclined his head toward the waitress who was walking toward us with a huge grin on her face.

"Not a word." Charlie's tone made it clear that if Matt gave him crap about this, there would be hell to pay.

"Hi, I'm Clarissa, and I'm waiting on this section. Are you ready to order?"

"Chili-cheese fries and a Coke," I said.

Clarissa smiled at Charlie and her cheeks turned pink. "Did you need anything else?"

"No, thanks," Charlie said, avoiding eye contact.

The girl's smile wavered. "Okay then. I'll be right out with those fries."

When she was far enough away that she couldn't hear, I said, "Is your plan to ignore her until she asks you on a date? 'Cause I don't think that's going to work."

Matt snorted. "I told him to ask for her number."

"I'm working up to it," Charlie said.

My home life may be a mess, but I didn't usually have

trouble talking to girls.

"West, what are you doing here?" Nina's voice came from behind me.

I turned to see her standing there with her friend. Of course, she was wearing a Harry Potter shirt, which was bookishly hot. "I'm here offering moral support to my cousin Charlie so he'll grow some balls and ask Clarissa on a date."

Nina smiled and glanced back and forth between my cousins. "I'm guessing you're Charlie, since you look like you want to punch West."

"That's hardly a test, since he always looks like he wants to punch someone," Matt said.

Clarissa came toward us carrying my order on a bright orange tray. Her smile faltered when she saw our group had grown by two girls.

"Here you go." She set the tray on the table. "Anyone need anything else?"

"Clarissa, have you met Charlie?" Nina asked.

I barely suppressed a laugh at the panicked look on Charlie's face.

"I've seen him around school," Clarissa said. "Why do you ask?"

"I think he likes you, but he's too shy to ask for your number," Nina said.

"Well, if he ever works up the nerve, I'd probably give it to him." Clarissa grinned and then walked off.

"See," Nina said. "Nothing to worry about."

Charlie leaned over and punched me on the shoulder.

"What was that for?" I asked.

"Your girlfriend is the one giving me grief," he said.

"She's not my girlfriend," I said.

"Nope," Nina said. "I'm just the girl he's taking to the Valentine's Day Dance."

"We're not going to that stupid dance," I said.

"You could ask Clarissa to the dance," Nina said to Charlie. "We could double, since West and I are absolutely going to the dance."

Matt laughed. "I like her. She doesn't take any crap, and she tries to boss you around."

"Yes," I said. "She's a ray of sunshine."

"You know you like me." Nina sat next to me and stole one of my fries.

I did like her, but I still felt the need to give her some grief. "Well, help yourself, why don't you?"

She grinned and snatched another fry. "Okay."

I rolled my eyes. "I thought you were fluent in sarcasm."

Chapter Nineteen

Nina

"I helped out your cousin, and I'm taking my due in french fries."

"I like you." West pulled his fries closer like he was defending his territory. "But chili-cheese fries are my favorite food on the planet."

"Fine." I laughed. "I'll order my own."

"I'll get them," Charlie said. "Since apparently, I'm going to talk to Clarissa, anyway."

"Good for you." I did a small happy dance in my seat.

West looked at me like I was insane.

"What? I helped and I'm happy about it."

"No. You stuck your nose in where it didn't belong," West said. "And it just happened to work out. What if she didn't like him?"

"But she did." I pretended to reach for one of his fries.

He sighed and pushed the container toward me. "You're lucky I like you."

Matt pointed at Lisa. "You can sit, if you want to."

"I was waiting to see how Nina's meddling turned out before I committed to taking a seat. We've had to make some quick exits in the past."

"Imagine my surprise," West said.

"That was only one time," I said. "And I had no idea the guy was dating two girls."

Charlie came back with a container of chili-cheese fries and a smile on his face.

"Did she give you her number?" I asked.

"Yes," he said.

Lisa sat down between Matt and me and reached for one of the fries. "I call dibs on the fries without chili."

"They're chili-cheese fries," Matt said. "That's the whole point."

Lisa shrugged. "I prefer the cheese."

"So you could order cheese fries," Matt said.

"Allow me to explain," I said. "If we share fries, then we can pretend we're eating semi-healthy because we didn't scarf down a whole order of fries by ourselves. It's a girl thing."

"Shouldn't you be drinking diet soda while you eat the fries?" Matt said. "My sister thinks that cancels out the calories."

"Makes sense, but no, because diet soda is gross," I said. "If I'm going to drink the chemicals, I'd rather have the flavor, too."

We ate our fries and made small talk until the theme song for *Harry Potter* blasted through the speakers and the television flickered to life. Someone dimmed the lights. "Time to relocate for a better view."

I tossed my empty fries container. Lisa and I headed back over to the table we'd staked out with our coats.

"Matt is cute," Lisa said. "And he's not nearly as moody as West."

"I think he just likes giving me crap. If this were a novel, the love of a good woman would save West and turn him into a happier person"

"I'm pretty sure that only happens in books," Lisa said. "In real life, if you're unhappy, you need to work to change yourself. Having someone who cares about you helps, but it's not a magic anti-jerk pill."

"That sounded profound until the anti-jerk-pill part." Out of the corner of my eye, I saw West and his friends approaching. They joined us at our table. West sat next to me.

"I'm sorry. Are you lost?" I asked. He'd given me trouble, so I felt the need to return the favor.

"Clarissa gets off work in half an hour, and she wants to watch the movie with Charlie, which apparently means Matt and I are also watching *Harry Potter.*"

I leaned over and whispered. "Have you figured out what you're wearing to the Valentine's Dance?"

"No. Because we're not going," he said.

I elbowed him in the ribs. "Yes we are."

"I'm trying to watch the movie," West said. "Please keep your delusional thoughts to yourself."

I inched my chair closer so my arm was touching his. He looked at me, like he was wondering what I was up to. I batted my eyelashes at him and grinned. He rolled his eyes, but then he put his arm around my shoulders.

Score one for the bookworms of the world. I leaned into him, enjoying the warmth. I ignored reality and watched the movie. It wasn't long until Clarissa came and joined Charlie at the table. They made a cute couple. The setup could have been awkward for Matt and Lisa, but neither of them seemed bothered by the situation. I envied Lisa's laid-back attitude about life. Where I liked to argue and wear people down, she tended to flow along with the tide. Nothing really bothered her. Matt seemed fairly relaxed. Maybe they'd make a good couple.

They say opposites attract. West and I were certainly opposites. I liked my life full of dog fur and stacks of books. He just wanted to cut down on things that could collect dust. I still couldn't believe his attitude toward the Hilmer Library. Maybe I could do something to change his mind.

We watched the movie in silence, but I was hyperaware of his arm around my shoulders and the warmth of his touch. I wanted to turn my face to his to see if he would kiss me.

It had been a few days since he'd done anything but make small talk. The rational part of my brain reminded me that even though West may be a hottie and he might smell good, that didn't mean he was the guy for me. Somewhere out there, there was probably a guy who owned a massive library, just waiting for me to show up so we could talk books. If I was smart, I'd play it cool with West and be on the lookout for a guy who dreamed of building a house with floor-to-ceiling bookshelves.

Rather than think big thoughts, I let myself get lost in the magic of Hogwarts. When the movie wrapped up, West moved his arm from around my shoulders. Now what? Why did that seem to be the daily question around him?

He moved his chair away from mine and took a drink of his soda. "Nothing like a wild and crazy Saturday night of watching *Harry Potter.*"

"Charlie and Clarissa seem to be hitting it off," I said.

Lisa scooted closer. "Matt asked if I'd give him a ride home so he doesn't have to butt in on his brother's date. I figured since West was here, he could give you a ride."

"What do you think?" I asked him, not wanting to presume anything and jinx the situation.

"It's not far," he said. "You could walk."

Chapter Twenty

"I could," Nina said. "But then I might trip over my own feet walking up the driveway, bump into your driver's-side mirror, and knock it off. Accidentally, of course."

"Not funny," I said. Even though it was a little funny. "I guess I can give you a ride home."

"Thank you."

Once everyone had his or her ride situation taken care of, Nina followed me out to my car.

She examined the repaired passenger door mirror. "Good as new."

"Let's keep it that way." I climbed into the car and hit the automatic unlock so she could get in.

"Your cousins seem nice," she said.

Was she trying to make conversation, or was she saying she was interested in them? Charlie appeared to be off the market, but Matt was still single. The idea of Nina with either of them made the chili cheese fries I'd eaten shift around in my gut. "Yeah. They're good guys."

"Maybe Lisa and Matt will hit it off," she said.

"Doubtful. Matt isn't really interested in dating one girl."

"Why not?" she asked.

"I don't know. He seems to date around."

Nina's phone buzzed with a text. She sucked in a breath like she was excited about something. Had some guy texted her?

"I don't suppose I could talk you into swinging by the bookstore?" she said with a hopeful look on her face. "A book I ordered came in."

She was that excited about a book? That was nerdily cute, and it's not like I had anything better to do. "Sure. What's the book?"

"It's the third book in a dystopian romance, and I've been waiting on it for a year."

"A romance?"

"Oh, please. All books have romance in them. You can't tell me you weren't waiting for Ron to kiss Hermione."

"Nope. I wasn't."

"Sure you weren't. I think guys and book snobs are afraid to admit romance is part of every book and everyone's life. Too bad it works out so much better in books than in real marriages."

She sounded more cynical about the whole romance thing than most females I knew. "I thought all girls believed in love and happily ever after."

"I used to believe in that, and then I found out my dad had another wife and family."

Well, hell. What did I say to that? We'd reached the bookstore, so I pulled in and parked. "Your dad had another family?"

She nodded. "Yep. A wife and two kids while he was still married to my mom."

"Okay. You can be as cynical as you want."

"The real kicker is the other kids were so much younger than us. Like we weren't the family he wanted, so he decided to start over."

"Did the second family know about you and your mom?" I asked.

"No. He'd lied to her, too, though she stayed with him for a while and tried to make it work. After she kicked him out, he called my mom to complain."

"That's ballsy," I said. "Or really stupid."

She nodded. "My mom never told me, but I think he asked if he could come back."

"But your mom was too smart for that."

"Thank goodness. I don't know how she could trust him or how any of us could after he'd lied...literally, for years."

"Which is why you insist on always telling the truth." It all made sense now.

"Yes." She glanced over at me. "Lisa is the only other person who knows about this, so I'd appreciate it if you kept it to yourself."

"I can do that."

The fierce expression Nina normally wore was gone. She looked sort of sad and deflated.

"The reason your dad started another family is not because there was anything wrong with any of you. It's because there was something wrong with him."

"I wish I could believe that," she said.

I couldn't believe I was about to say this, but it felt like the right thing to do. "You need a hug, don't you?"

"Yes."

I unbuckled my seat belt and moved toward her. She met me halfway. Putting my arms around her and pulling her close felt natural. We fit together easily. The apple-mint scent of her hair invaded my senses, reminding me of the last time we'd been this close in a parking lot, where I'd planned on kissing her until that car honked and messed things up.

Right now, I wanted to comfort her, but there was more to it than that. I wanted to touch her. Sitting at Bixby's with my arm around her shoulders had felt right. And now, I wanted to kiss her. Before I could put my plan into motion, Nina released me.

"Thanks, I needed that." She turned and opened the car door, so I followed her across the parking lot, trying to think of something to say that might make her feel better about her family. In a weird way, her confession made me feel better about my own situation. My mom might be mental, but my dad had stayed by her side. He could have left her, could have left me to deal with the craziness by myself while he found someone else to marry. I'd never thought of it like that before. My respect for him went up a few notches.

We entered the store, which smelled like coffee and cookies. It had been forever since I'd been in a real bookstore. There were rows upon rows of books and a large clearance section. Surprisingly, there was a line at the front desk.

"I think they're texting everyone to come pick up their books. You can look around while I wait in line."

I didn't need any books. I could buy anything I wanted on my Kindle. But I was here, so I might as well look. "I'll check out the clearance section." There were several aisles of discounted books. Some new and some used. A science fiction book I'd been meaning to read caught my eye. Nina's comment about losing all digital content if there was an EMP blast came to mind. Maybe having a few paperbacks on hand wasn't a terrible idea.

Then again, bringing anything into my house was a bad idea. I regularly had nightmares where my house sank into the ground from all the excess weight of my mother's hoard. I put the book back and headed toward the checkout line to join Nina.

"You didn't find anything?" She seemed surprised. "How is that possible?"

"I found a few things but nothing I couldn't live without," I said.

She shook her head. "You either have way too much will power, or you're a tiny bit crazy."

"Probably both," I said.

"Normal is overrated." She grinned at me and then moved forward to the next open cashier.

Chapter Twenty-One

NINA

After I paid for my book, I followed West back out to his car. Telling him the truth about my family had felt freeing. Once we were on the road again, I said, "It's kind of nice that you know the truth about my family. It's cool that I can share things with you and you understand."

"I'm the last person to judge anyone's messed-up family," he said.

"Do you ever think that everyone is just pretending and those perfect families you see on television don't actually exist."

"I think every family has issues," he said. "Some are bigger or stranger or sadder than others."

Which one of those categories did he place his own home life in? It's not like I could ask, but I suspected he classified his situation as sad. Not that I could blame him.

Unable to resist, I cracked my book and started reading. I didn't realize we were in the driveway until West put the car in park and said, "Earth to Nina."

"Sorry." I slid the receipt between the pages to mark my place. "Thanks for giving me a ride." And suddenly it seemed awkward. Was this a date? Would he ever try to kiss me again? Should I just go?

His phone buzzed and he checked it, which gave me an easy out. "See you later."

"See ya," He continued reading his text, and I climbed out of the car, intent on hiding away in my room for a marathon reading session.

Sunday was a glorious day. I read my book on the couch, between doing loads of laundry. My mom hated laundry, and my brother was banned from touching the washer and dryer since he shrank a load of my mom's good blouses by drying them on high. I found laundry cathartic, and I loved the smell of dryer sheets.

The only part I didn't like was schlepping the clean clothes upstairs to our bedrooms. We used to live in a ranch house where everything was on one floor.

I was folding a load of towels, which were still warm from the dryer, when my cell buzzed. Lisa's mom had told her there was a rally to raise money to keep the Hilmer Library open. It was scheduled for later today. I bet West and his social studies teacher didn't know about that. Lisa planned to pick me up in a few hours.

The meeting was at a donut shop near the library. On the plus side, the owner gave us free bear claws. On the negative side, Lisa and I were the youngest people in the room by about twenty years. Where were all the other high-school-aged bookworms?

"We are racing against the clock, ladies," the speaker

said. "A rehab date has been set. They plan to pretty much gut the place and turn it into a recycling center. We still might have a chance to keep the library open until the new one is completed, but we need to get the word out. We've handed out fliers, but we need another approach. Any ideas?"

I raised my hand. "There's a social studies teacher who is giving students extra credit for helping with projects that help the community. One of the projects is volunteering to help salvage things from the library before the building is rehabbed. Why can't we start a group for extra credit to help keep the library open?"

"It can't hurt," the speaker said. "My daughter-in-law, Mrs. Stone, is an English teacher at the high school." She pulled out her cell. "Give me a moment."

After a quick conversation, the speaker said, "My daughter-in-law is going to talk to the social studies department about asking students to help maintain the library as one of their extra credit projects."

If the social studies teacher agreed, this could be awesome. West could get extra credit for keeping the library open, instead of working to turn it into a recycling center.

"Any other ideas?" the woman asked.

Several women offered to pass out more fliers, and a few offered to do an informational picket line. Lisa and I volunteered to pass out fliers at school. Who knew? Maybe we could make a difference.

• • •

When I went home, Gidget met me at the door, transmitting joy and happiness. "I'm happy to see you, too."

No one else seemed to be home, so I curled up on the couch with Gidget and my book. An hour later, my mom came in the front door, and she wasn't alone. She was with the one person I never wanted to see again. I stared at the man who'd thrown us away.

"Hi, Nina."

"Hello, Dad." He looked a little worse for wear. His shirt was wrinkled, like he'd slept in it, and there were dark circles under his eyes. "What a surprise." And not a pleasant one. I looked at my mom for some sort of explanation.

"He needed my signature to sell his car," Mom said.

I laughed. "Of course. Because it's not like he'd come to visit, since he doesn't give a crap about any of us."

"Nina." My dad came toward me but stopped short of touching me. "You know I still care about you."

Anger surged inside of me like a geyser. "How? How would I know that? When was the last time you made an effort to speak to Jason or me?"

He blinked and looked down at the carpet. "There's no excuse for what I did, but it wasn't about you and your brother, or even your mom. It was my issue."

"Yeah, well your issue screwed up our lives. And saying you're a shitty person doesn't make up for the damage you did."

"Nina." My mom's voice was gentle. "He'll be gone in five minutes. I promise. Believe me, I don't want him here either."

I couldn't deal with this, so I headed out the back door. How could my mom even be in the same room with him? I stalked past the patio furniture and kept walking.

I hated the way he made me feel—angry and worthless. And his it's-not-you-it's-me excuse was total crap. Nervous energy buzzed through my veins like electricity, so I kept walking past the shed and past West's barbecue court. I wove through some evergreen trees and came to a halt at the fence that marked the end of our property. No, not our property... West's family's property. My anger circled around again. My dad was the reason we were stuck renting. Who knew if we'd ever have our own house again?

I grabbed the top metal bar of the chain-link fence and stared past it. A field separated us from the houses in the next subdivision. Nothing to see out here. Now what? And why hadn't I thought to grab a coat? Goose bumps broke out on my arms. I released the cold metal fence and hugged myself for warmth.

"Nina?"

I turned around. "West? What are you doing out here?"

"You stole my line." He came closer. "Are you okay?"

"No." And I didn't want to talk about it. I'd managed not to cry up to this point, but if I talked about it, the angry tears might make a break for it.

"I was about to start a fire, if you want to come sit with me."

"Thanks. I'd like that." I followed him back to the overgrown basketball court. The barbecue pit was full of paper covered with charcoal. I sat in one of the lawn chairs and pulled my knees up to my chest.

West sat and scooted his lawn chair close to mine. "Do you want to talk about it?"

I studied his face. Concern shone from his bright blue eyes. He really did care. But talking about it wouldn't change anything. "Can I have a hug instead?"

"Sure." He wrapped his arms around me. I closed my eyes and sighed, trying to let my cares slide away. It wasn't working. I needed a distraction. And there happened to be a handsome, masculine-smelling hottie-of-a-distraction right in front of me. I repositioned myself so my mouth lined up with his and waited to see if he'd play along.

A cold wet splat landed on the top of my head. I jerked backward. "What the hell?"

Big, fat raindrops splattered all around us. "Seriously?" Like I needed to be rained on right now.

"Come on." West grabbed my hand and we ran through the rain until we reached the overhang of the shed.

And now we had a problem. "I'm not ready to go back in my house yet, and we can't go in yours. I mean you could go in yours…" I hoped he wouldn't leave me.

"If I show you something, you can't make fun of me," West said.

"Okay." This should be interesting.

He turned and opened the shed door, waving me inside. With the click of a light switch, I understood what West had meant. The shed was more like a playroom. Or at least half of it was. A love seat with a *Teenage Mutant Ninja Turtles* blanket sat against one wall. And there was a bookshelf stacked with books, puzzles, board games, a radio, and a few model cars. There was a small refrigerator plugged into the wall. Boxes of Pop-Tarts and protein bars were stacked on top. The other half of the shed had storage boxes, shelves for tools, and a lawnmower.

"What is this place?" I asked.

He went over and sat on the love seat, so I joined him. "This is the last bit of normalcy from when I was ten, before my mom became sick. We used to keep all these games in the living room. My mom loved to play. And then things changed. I moved the games out here because I always hoped one day she'd want to play again. That never happened, but I couldn't bring myself to throw all these things away. I come out here to read sometimes. I know the Ninja Turtle blanket is ridiculous." He pointed at the refrigerator. "But I do have soda and strawberry Pop-Tarts."

I could picture a ten-year-old kid, hoping his family would become normal again, trying to preserve something that was special. And now I wanted to cry for West. "I'm so sorry about your mom."

He shrugged. "It is what it is. So what were you running

away from?"

He'd confessed, so it wasn't like I could blow him off and not give an answer. "My jackass of a father stopped by, but not because he missed us or wanted to catch up. He came by because he needed my mom to sign off on selling his car. And when I called him on that, he played the, it's-not-you-it's-me card. And I hate him." My voice broke. "I hate how he makes me feel."

"Like your life is out of control and the grown-ups running everything don't really know what the hell they're doing?" West guessed.

"Well yes...but I meant how he makes me feel...like trash...because he threw us away."

West stared at me for a moment, and then he said, "That is ridiculous."

My face heated. "That's what it feels like."

"This is one of those hugging moments, isn't it?" He rolled his eyes. "It's totally your fault that I now think this way."

"I'll take complete credit." I met him halfway, but the hug was awkward. I shifted around on the loveseat and our faces lined up. This was it. The do-or-die moment. He'd either kiss me, or consign me to the friend zone. I stared into his eyes, looking for a clue.

His warm breath feathered across my lips, making me hyperaware of how close he was, how good this could be.

"West?" I murmured, hoping he'd understand what I was asking, what I wanted.

The corners of his mouth turned up in a small, sexy smile, and then he kissed me. His lips were warm and soft. The sound of the rain hitting the shed roof faded into the background as his mouth moved against mine. I threw myself into the moment. Nothing mattered except the sensation of his mouth pressed against mine, and the warmth growing between us. Unlike the car, there was no reason to stop, no car horn to honk and break us apart.

The sensation of his hands skimming under the back of my shirt, his palm pressed against the small of my back, sent a wave of heat through my body, making it difficult to think. But I didn't want to think. I just wanted to hide away from the world with him. Being in his arms like this helped drain away the anger…helped me focus on the good things in my life.

Chapter Twenty-Two

No one beyond my dad, Matt, and Charlie knew about my hideaway in the shed. Being here with Nina felt right. I wasn't embarrassed about it like I probably should have been. The fact that she just accepted it—accepted me—made my world a brighter place.

We kissed for a while and then she pulled away. Her cheeks were flushed and her eyes were bright. "Thanks for sharing this with me." She looked past me toward the bookshelf. "Is that what I think it is?"

I knew exactly what she was talking about. Reaching over I snagged my copy of *Harry Potter*. "It is." I held it out to her. The rain sounded like it was still coming down in sheets. "Do you want to read it?"

"We could read it together," she said.

"How?"

"We could sit here, like this." She scooted closer. "Put your arm around my shoulder, and I'll hold the book so we can both see it."

I almost made fun of the idea, but vulnerability shone in Nina's eyes, like she knew she was taking a chance. "Okay."

She snuggled against me, and I inhaled her apple-mint shampoo smell.

"Ready?" she asked.

"What if we read at different speeds?" I asked.

"Like most things in life, we'll figure it out as we go along," she said. "Or we could take turns reading out loud."

No one had read aloud to me in forever. The idea made me smile. "Okay. You start."

Nina read, and I found myself listening to the way she said the words, rather than what she was saying. She threw herself into the story, totally immersing herself in that world. She paused and glanced at my face. "What?"

I shrugged. "Nothing…you're good at this."

"At reading out loud?" She seemed to doubt my sincerity.

"Yes." And that was the nerdiest compliment I'd ever given anyone.

"If I tell you something," she said, "do you promise not to laugh at me?"

"You didn't give me crap about the Ninja Turtles blanket, so you're good."

"I think it would be cool to be a narrator for audiobooks."

"That *would* be cool." I pulled the book from her hands. "But I think it's time to take a break."

"A break?" She pretended not to know that I wanted to kiss her. She pointed at the board games. "Are you in the mood for Yahtzee?"

"Not exactly." I pulled her close. "Guess again."

"Go Fish?" she said, right before I brushed my lips across hers.

"You're really bad at guessing," I teased before I kissed her again. And then we stopped talking. Everything sort of fell into place, like it was natural for us to make out on the love seat during a rainstorm. Like we sort of belonged together. And I needed to stop thinking about this before I freaked myself out.

A little while later, Nina stopped kissing me and tilted her head to the side. "What's wrong?" I asked.

"I think the rain stopped."

I listened. She was right. "Does that mean you want to leave?" It's not like we were trapped together any longer, but I didn't want her to go.

In response, she just shook her head. "But I could use a snack. Or we could go to my house for real food, if you want."

I needed a reason for us not to go to her house, because even though I didn't want her to leave, going to her house would feel too...domestic or relationship-ish. "I'm in the mood for Italian food. Do you want to go grab a calzone somewhere?"

"Sure. I'll meet you at your car in twenty minutes."

My father gave me an odd look when I came in through the back door. "Nina and I are going to grab something to eat."

Hanging out with Nina was easy, even comfortable. Maybe because she'd told me her family's secrets, which made me realize all families have issues. I wanted to tell her the truth about my mom, but it didn't seem like the right time.

And it's not like I was pretending my family was perfect. She knew it was messed up. She just didn't know my mom's illness was psychological rather than physical.

When Nina joined me at my car, she was frowning.

"What's wrong?" I asked.

"Let's talk on the way," she said.

"Okay." I started my Fusion, and we backed out of the driveway. I waited for her to start talking. At the first stop light we came to, I said, "Should I ask questions or do you need time to think?"

She slid lower in her seat. "Most of the time I can keep a lid on my anger and pretend everything is okay. Then my dad shows up and my self-control goes out the window. My mom can keep her cool around him. I can't. Even though he's gone and he probably won't be back, my house doesn't feel right anymore. Does that make sense?"

"You're saying he's like a skunk that stinks up your house with toxic anger-creating fumes?"

She laughed, which is what I'd been aiming for.

"Yes. Exactly like that."

Nina seemed more her normal self at the restaurant. We talked about books and television shows we liked. Then the topic of school came up.

"It doesn't make sense for both of us to drive when we're going to the same place." She sipped her coffee and waited for my response.

If I didn't offer to give her a ride, she probably wouldn't be interested in kissing me again. So even though it felt like I was being manipulated, I said, "We can ride together if you want."

"Sure." She beamed.

Maybe I was finally figuring this girlfriend thing out. Wait a minute. Why had I thought that? She wasn't my girlfriend. We were just...wait...I had no idea what we were doing. We'd passed the friendship stage, I was sure of that...so I guess we were dating. It's not like we were not-dating.

Nina pointed at my forehead. "Why are your eyebrows doing that?"

"Doing what?" I reached up to touch my face.

"They were squished together like you were irritated or in deep thought. Are you stressing out about giving me a ride to school?"

"No." It was much bigger than that. "I was trying to remember if I needed to stop by the store on the way home."

"I think you need to stock the shed with chocolate Pop-Tarts. The strawberry kind are good, but chocolate are my favorite."

"Why am I not surprised?"

. . .

Nina and I fell into a comfortable pattern. I gave her a ride to school every morning and then she went off to her locker to hang out with Lisa while I met up with Charlie and Matt.

"How did you make this happen?" Matt asked.

"What do you mean?"

"I always see guys walking girls to their lockers and hanging out with them rather than hanging with their own friends," Matt said. "You and Nina don't do that."

Huh. We'd never really talked about it. "Maybe because we hang out after school."

"See," Matt said. "Dating your neighbor is smart. It creates a less clingy girlfriend."

There was that word again.

"Dude, did you just flinch?" Charlie asked.

Had I? "Maybe. We haven't really labeled our... relationship status yet."

"I'm sure you have," Charlie said. "You just don't know it."

"Have you grown a pair and talked to Clarissa lately?" I asked. "Or do you need Nina to do it for you?"

Matt laughed.

No reason for me to be the lone target.

"At least I'm not sitting on the sidelines trying to wait out someone else's relationship," Charlie shot back.

Matt went very still, and I was pretty sure Charlie was about ten seconds from a broken nose.

Instead of exploding, Matt stalked off.

"Charlie, what did you do?" I asked.

He reached up and rubbed the back of his neck. "I messed up."

"Yes, you did, and good luck with that." Charlie was always the first to throw a punch, but when Matt was angry he stayed that way for a good long time.

• • •

Thursday on the drive home from school, Nina's cell buzzed. She checked it and grinned. Then she looked over at me. "Okay, this may sound like a bad thing, but it's not."

"No one has ever said that and meant it," I joked.

"Well, Lisa and I signed up for an extra-credit project, and you could sign up for it, too."

"I have an extra-credit project already."

"Yes, but this is a better option. There are people trying to keep the Hilmer Library open until the new building is finished, and now it's an option for extra credit."

Why is she doing this to me? "So, your extra-credit project directly clashes with mine."

"It's not like you actually want to turn that old building into a recycling center."

"Yes. I do."

"But...isn't it better to keep the library open and use something else for the recycling center, some place that is already a warehouse?"

I pointed out the obvious. "Recycling centers are good things. They help save the environment."

"Libraries help people, too."

"There are other libraries."

"How can you not see my idea is better?"

"Your argument is invalid. Just because you think it's a better idea doesn't mean it's actually a better idea." The more I talked about this, the more annoyed I became. "And before you come back at me with another ridiculous argument, just know this is not open to debate."

We didn't talk for the rest of the car ride home. She didn't say good-bye when she climbed out of the car and stalked over to her house.

Chapter Twenty-Three

NINA

"I don't get it," I griped to my mom and brother at dinner that night. "How can he not see this is a better option?"

"Maybe he's annoyed that you're working against him," Jason said.

"I'm not working against him. This isn't personal. And I have the moral high ground." My mom gave me the look, which meant she didn't quite agree with me.

"I need you to listen to me," my mom said. "Libraries are wonderful, but recycling centers are good, too. He doesn't want to bulldoze the building; he wants to convert it and give it another life."

"I get that." And really, I did. "But there are plenty of empty buildings that could be turned into a recycling center. Why close the library?"

"I don't know. But you two seemed to be doing well before this happened. Ask yourself this, is it something worth fighting over?"

Ugh. This was so frustrating. "I wasn't trying to start a fight; I just thought I was presenting him with a more logical option, and he won't even consider it."

"Maybe you need to respect his decision," Jason said. "I know you love to argue, but sometimes it's irritating."

"You can agree to disagree," my mom said. "Or if it's a deal breaker, then it's a deal breaker. You're the only one who can figure that out."

• • •

The next morning, I glanced out the picture window and spotted West sitting in his car, reading on his phone. I guess that meant he would give me a ride, if I still wanted one. Or maybe it meant he was reading a good book. This was going to be fabulously awkward.

My mom came up behind me and said, "Nothing ventured, nothing gained."

"How does that apply to this situation?"

"I think you're good for him, and I bet you could help him be a happier person."

"So he's a fixer-upper?" I asked.

"Most men are," she said. "And unless he moves or his dad evicts us, you're going to be spending time around him. See if you can get him to loosen up and live a little."

"I guess I'll give it a shot." *Bookworm versus Brooding Hottie who plots to close libraries, take two.*

When I opened the car door, he glanced up at me. "I wasn't sure if we were riding together today or not."

Okay. Was he saying he didn't want to give me a ride? "I'm not sure how to respond to that statement."

"It's simple," he said. "You either get in the car, or you close the door and drive yourself."

Okay then. At this point, I was leaning toward driving

myself. Or maybe I should ride with him for spite. Then again, did I want to deal with him being crabby this morning? I might be responsible for part of his mood, but it couldn't be all me.

"Just get in," he said with great irritation, as if he had the authority to tell me what to do. Wrong.

"Nope. I'm out." I slammed the door and walked up the driveway toward my car. Why should I put up with him being moody?

I heard his car door open and close, and then footsteps coming up behind me as I opened my car door.

"Nina, you're being ridiculous."

"Am I?" I turned to face him and crossed my arms over my chest. "I hate to break it to you, but the ratio of obnoxious to attractive is not working in your favor this morning."

He scrunched his eyebrows together. "What does that mean?"

I glared at him. "It's simple. The more obnoxious a person is, the less attractive he is. You wanting to close down the library, combined with not giving a crap whether I ride with you or not, has made you fairly unattractive."

He tilted his head and studied me for a moment. I waited for him to say something, but he didn't. The silence stretched out.

"Do you have a response?" I asked. "Are we done? Can I get in my car?"

He took a step toward me and then glanced back at his house. In a surprise move, he grabbed my arm. "Come with me."

Okay. Now what?

I allowed him to lead me around to the back of the shed where we weren't in view of anybody driving by on the street. He continued holding my arm, pulling me close so we were toe-to-toe.

My heart beat faster as he stared down at me and reached to brush my hair behind my ear. "So you're not attracted to me anymore, is that what you're saying?"

My brain said yes, but my hormones were too busy noticing that he smelled good, like clothes fresh from the dryer, combined with masculine shower gel.

Before I could answer, he leaned in and skimmed his mouth down the side of my neck. Heat shot through my body. My brain disengaged. "Oh…" was the most intelligent counterargument I could come up with.

He wrapped one arm around my waist. His lips skimmed across my earlobe. "You were saying."

Blood pounded through my veins so loudly he could probably hear my heartbeat. And I could feel the smugness radiating off his body, or maybe that was hormonal heat. "You're still wrong about closing the library," I said, before turning to line my mouth up with his.

"How can you—" he started to argue.

I cut off his argument by kissing him. For a second, I was afraid he'd push me away, like this had all been a joke. Then he took a step toward me, pressing my back against the wall of the shed. Suddenly, nothing else seemed important.

His mouth moved away from mine. "So this is you not wanting me?"

My face burned. "Fine. You're obnoxious and wrong about the library, but I still find you attractive."

"Then, I win." He grinned like he was quite proud of himself, and then he kissed me again, a slow, deep kiss that scrambled what was left of my brain. And then he left…just walked away from me and headed back toward the driveway and presumably toward his car. I heard the sound of his engine starting, followed by him driving away.

What. The. Hell? Had he just left me? I stalked around the shed to the driveway and stared at the spot where West's car should have been. Where he should have been waiting to smirk at me, because obviously I was still attracted to him, but that was okay because he was just as obviously still attracted to me. Which in my brain meant we were actually dating, which meant he should be giving me a ride to school. Apparently, my brain and my body were both idiots. And West was a complete jackass.

Chapter Twenty-Four

WEST

And the win goes to West. Where did she get off judging me, condemning me for wanting to help convert a building into a recycling center? It's not like I wanted to burn the place to the ground while orphans and puppies were trapped inside.

Besides, she'd been all talk. When it came down to it, she was still interested in me. I pulled into an open spot in the Greenbrier High parking lot and turned off the ignition. Doubt crept into my brain. I'd been so annoyed by her attitude—her judging me—and I wanted to prove her wrong. I'd won the argument, but maybe I should've waited to see if she changed her mind about the ride.

Too late for second thoughts now. Besides, it's not like I'd left her stranded somewhere. She had her own car. I watched the entrance to the parking lot, expecting to see her pull in. I checked my cell. It was earlier than she normally would've come to school. Maybe she'd gone back to her house for a cup of coffee or to make a voodoo doll. For a brief moment, I considered calling her, but if she was mad, and the odds were high, I'd get an earful. Better to let her cool off and talk to her later.

I climbed out of my car and walked across the gravel parking lot. Students hung out in groups by their cars, talking and laughing. A few people looked up as I walked by. Most ignored me. Some acknowledged me with a nod or a smile. I nodded back and kept moving. I didn't need to be sucked into anymore drama this morning.

Matt and Charlie waited for me by our lockers.

"Where's Nina?" Matt said.

"Why do you ask?"

Charlie glanced at Matt and then back at me. "You're dating, right? Or did you screw that up already?"

"We're sort of dating. That doesn't mean we have to ride to school together every day."

Matt sighed. "Nice going, Charlie. Now you've made him cranky."

"Shut up." I shoved some books in my locker and pulled out the ones I'd need before lunch.

"Incoming," Charlie said.

I turned around and saw Nina heading my way. She didn't break stride when she spotted me; she looked right through me like I wasn't even there and kept on going down the hall.

"Dude, you are screwed," Matt said.

"Royally," Charlie added. "And if you like that girl, you better do something to fix it fast because she's plotting revenge."

"You don't know that," I snapped.

"When a girl looks through you like that," Matt said, "she's not happy."

"Okay. Maybe I messed up." I told them about kissing Nina and walking away.

"Why didn't you stick around and give her a ride?" Matt

asked.

"She said she'd drive herself." I shrugged. "It made sense at the time." Now not so much.

"And you were being an over-competitive jerk," Charlie added.

"Yes, I know, but thanks for pointing that out," I said. Maybe I should talk to Nina and try to apologize. Then again, there was no reason for me to approach her during the school day. If she was going to freak out, she could do it away from all the gossips. "I'll talk to her after school."

I went about my day with a vague sense of unease. I'd acted like an idiot. I got that now. Sometimes when I was mad I made stupid decisions. Didn't everybody do that? By lunch, I was tired of feeling like a jerk, so I decided to suck it up and join Nina and Lisa at their table.

She watched my approach with a look of confusion and irritation. I set my tray down and said, "On a scale of I-want-to-yell-at-him to I-want-to-egg-his-car, how mad are you?"

Showing zero emotion, she said, "How mad do you think I should be?"

Lisa laughed between bites of her Twinkie.

Nothing was ever easy, especially with Nina. "I should have waited to see if you wanted a ride this morning," I said. "But in my defense, you were the one who said you'd drive yourself."

"That was before you kissed me under false pretenses."

I blinked at her. "This might piss you off more, but I have no idea what you mean."

She huffed out a breath. "Then you should go eat lunch someplace else."

"Fine." I pushed to my feet. "I tried."

"Yeah, that's what every girl wants to hear." She shook her head. "And just so you know, I won't be riding to school with you anymore."

That shouldn't have bothered me as much as it did. Whatever. I headed back over to sit with Matt and Charlie.

"You made it worse, didn't you?" Matt said.

"Doesn't matter," I said. "It's over."

"And now you have to see her every day," Charlie said. "That's going to suck."

"Not a big deal," I said. "She'll go back to being my neighbor." No problem. No problem at all.

Chapter Twenty-Five

NINA

I watched West walk away from me.

"Emotionally stunted jerkwad," Lisa muttered.

"I was thinking more along the lines of idiotic jackass, but jerkwad works, too." I took a deep breath and blew it out. "I don't get it. Why would he kiss me like he cared about me and wanted me to be his girlfriend if he wasn't really interested?"

"Because he's a guy?" Lisa said. "I'm pretty sure the identity of the person they're kissing or doing other things with doesn't matter as much as the fact that they are involved in those activities."

"I sincerely hope that isn't true. There must be guys out there looking for the one special someone they want to spend the rest of their lives with. Right?"

"Maybe males in their late twenties," Lisa said. "But I doubt there's a single guy in high school who isn't looking to hook up with as many girls as possible."

"For someone whose mom is a therapist, you are really

jaded."

"Maybe that's why I'm jaded," she said. "I grew up playing in her office. I've seen way too many examples of how things can go wrong."

Lisa's dad had bailed before she was born. He was that special breed of asshole who took off when his wife became pregnant. Like suddenly, the demands of impending parenthood made marriage seem overwhelming. There was probably a designated area in hell for men who abandoned their pregnant wives. Next to the section for lying polygamists.

My cell dinged. Had West grown a conscience? I checked the text. Nope it was from the Hilmer Library committee. "Guess what we're doing this weekend?"

"Going to the bookstore," Lisa said.

"That's a given," I said. "But we are also going to the Hilmer Library to join the picketers protesting closing the library before the new one is ready. It's for a good cause, and it will annoy the ever-loving crap out of West."

"Then it's a win-win."

That night after school, I sat on the couch, trying to lose myself in a book, but my brain wasn't willing to let the question of West go. A cold, wet nose bumped my arm. Gidget wagged her tail with her eyes full of hope and a Frisbee clamped between her teeth.

"Do you want to play Frisbee?" I asked, just to see her reaction.

Gidget jumped up and down, doing a furry tap dance. Blonde fur flew in every direction and floated through the air. "You're the best dog."

I headed outside to the backyard to throw the Frisbee. Gidget ran and caught every throw. Watching her had me repeating my mantra. *Be more like the dog. Be happier in the moment.*

I tried to prevent my gaze from traveling to West's house.

Not easy to do since I was less than one hundred feet away. As usual, the whole house was dark. No. That wasn't quite right. Stark white light shone through the kitchen window, and a woman was standing there smiling at me. I smiled and waved at her. A look of panic crossed her face, and she disappeared from view.

Well, crap. I hadn't meant to traumatize her. It was just a wave. West's whole family must be mental.

I threw the Frisbee a dozen more times until Gidget lay down with the Frisbee by her side. "All done, girl?"

She panted in reply. I stretched out on the grass next to her and thought about West. He had tried to speak to me today, but that didn't make up for him ditching me, after kissing me like he wanted me as his girlfriend. I should have known this story wouldn't have a happily ever after. Brooding hotties didn't fall for bookworm hippie chicks. And bookworm hippie chicks shouldn't waste their time on boys who weren't emotionally available.

• • •

Over the next couple of days, I acknowledged West with a nod when I saw him, just like I had done before any of this mess ever happened. He nodded back. So the universe might be back in balance, but I didn't love the situation.

Saturday afternoon, Lisa and I met a dozen other people outside of Hilmer Library. We stood on the wide front steps of the building, passing out literature and collecting donations for the effort to keep the library open until the new building was complete.

"How many signatures do we need?" Lisa asked one of the organizers.

"As many as we can get," the woman said. "I'm hoping to stall the rehab until we can find a benefactor willing to help us speed up the completion of the new library. Excuse me, I see someone I need to talk to." The woman walked away.

Lisa frowned at me. "The odds do not seem like they are in our favor."

"At least we're trying," I said.

"Don't look now, but a certain jerkwad is coming your way."

I thought about asking which jerkwad she meant, but I knew who it was, even without Gidget there to bark at him.

"What's all this?" West asked, waving his hands around to indicate the dozen people handing out fliers and holding picket signs.

"This is free speech in action," I said. "I'm not the only one who thinks the library should stay open."

"The rehab date is set for next week," West said. "This is a waste of time. You're not going to stop it."

"Maybe if I chain myself to the front doors..." I was sort of joking.

"If you love this building so much, then why don't you help my friends and me salvage the woodwork? Then you'd be saving part of history without impeding progress."

Behind West, his cousins Matt and Charlie plus a few other guys I didn't know stood holding all sorts of tools. I recognized the crowbars and the saws but wasn't sure about some of the other stuff. Unfortunately, what they planned to do with those tools was clear.

"You can't just stroll in there and start ripping the place apart."

"Actually, we can. Mr. Stanton received notice that the books worth keeping have been boxed up and moved to storage, so we can start taking out the wainscoting and the doorframes." He pulled an envelope from his back pocket. "Who's in charge around here?"

"The lady in the blue jacket," I said.

West went over to the lady and showed her the letter. Her shoulders slumped in defeat and then she cleared her throat. "Everyone, these young men have a work order that allows them to salvage the contents of the building. We have to let them pass."

"Can we follow them inside?" I asked.

"As long as you stay out of our way," West answered.

"Don't mind us; we'll just be sitting on the floor in front of the wainscoting...maybe leaning on doorframes. I'm sure you'll be able to work around us." I smiled at him. "If anyone else wants to come inside with us, I'm sure we won't impede their progress."

A grandmotherly woman with steel gray hair turned and walked up the steps, taking her travel chair with her. She set the chair in the threshold of the doorway. "Oh, dear. I don't feel well. I better sit," she announced in a voice worthy of a soap opera.

Blue jacket woman carried her own chair up the steps and plopped down beside the other woman, effectively blocking the entrance. "Don't worry. I'll sit here with you until you feel better."

Both women looked at West. "Sorry. You'll have to find another entrance into the library."

Chapter Twenty-Six

I'd never been smirked at by someone old enough to be my grandmother. Since there was no way to fight back or respond to a woman in her sixties without looking like a total ass, I resorted to sarcasm. "Sorry you're not feeling well," I deadpanned. "Don't worry. We'll find another way inside."

Half the protesters, including Nina and her friend, ran around the side of the building, intent on blocking the other entries. Once again, nothing was ever simple. "Now what?"

"Come with me," Matt said with more confidence than the situation called for, unless he knew something I didn't. He led us to the side of the front steps where there was an area of latticework behind some overgrown bushes. He grabbed a section of the lattice and tugged on it. It popped off with a cracking sound.

"This is how horror movies start," I said.

"This is where the maintenance guy stored his lawn mower," Charlie informed me. "Plus there's a door into the basement."

"How do you know that?" I asked.

"We did the landscaping here a few years ago," Charlie said.

My cousins entered the dark, more than likely cobweb-infested area, without a second thought. I put on my work gloves and grabbed a flashlight from the toolbox because I wanted to see how filthy the area was before I walked into it. Weeds and cobwebs seemed woven together. Random tools and lawnmower parts littered the ground. The entire area looked like a tetanus shot or a trip to the emergency room waiting to happen.

"Watch out for rats," Matt called back to me.

He'd better be joking. I entered the pit of doom, swinging my flashlight around, trying to avoid the worst of the spider webs. I heard Charlie curse and the sound of metal screeching.

"Someone has jacked up this door." He tugged again and the door inched open.

Something dropped onto my head. I froze and then leaned forward and casually finger combed my hair while I fought the urge to flee out into the sunshine and fresh air.

I heard the sound of screeching metal again. "Got it," Charlie said.

Great. Because walking into a pitch-black basement was a smart life choice.

"What the hell is that smell?" Charlie called out.

"Forget it." Matt gagged and backed up. "We'll find another way.

The stench rolled out to greet me, and it was worse than anything I'd ever been exposed to, and that was saying something. I retreated back to the sunshine. Matt followed close behind me. He was coughing and Charlie looked green. "Dude, I think someone died in there."

"It was bad," Matt said, "but not that bad."

"No." Charlie bent over and took a deep breath. "I saw clothes and food wrappers like someone has been living there."

Hopefully, it had just been squatters who'd left a mess. I pulled out my cell. "We need to tell someone."

"Tell someone what?" Nina walked toward us, the amused expression slipping from her face.

"Looks like someone has been camping out in the basement," Charlie said. "And from the smell, they might have died there."

"Oh my God," Nina said. "What are you going to do?"

"I'm calling the police." If anyone specialized in dead bodies, it was them. I Googled the number and spoke to the woman who answered the phone. She said they'd send someone to investigate.

"Not that it compares to finding a dead body, but you have a wolf spider on your shoulder," Nina said.

I smacked the fuzzy gray spider on my shoulder, smashing the nickel-sized arachnid, which was disgusting. Thank God I had my work gloves on. It still felt like things were crawling on me. "Damn spiders." I pulled my sweatshirt off and shook it. Just to be sure, I turned it inside out and shook it again and then inspected every inch of it before putting it back on.

Nina was looking at me oddly.

"What?"

"Your hair," she said. "There's another one."

I bent over and shook my head. Sure enough a spider dropped from my head on a silk thread and hit the ground before scuttling away. I pulled off my gloves and ran my fingers through my hair again, hoping I didn't have any more surprise guests.

"Dude, you could never be a landscaper," Charlie said.

Matt laughed.

Whatever. "You can play in the dirt for the rest of your

lives if you want to, but I'm going to work in a nice clean office with lots of windows."

"Should we let the others know that the police are on their way?" Nina asked.

"That's probably a good idea."

She walked off toward the other picketers. Her friend Lisa hung back a minute. "Just so you know, you can still fix things with Nina, if you actually like her." And then she took off.

Matt and Charlie both looked at me like they were waiting for me to say something. "What?"

"She's still into you," Matt said.

Charlie nodded. "So what are you going to do about it?"

I pointed at the library. "Hello...possible dead body trumps dating issues."

The police arrived ten minutes later. It turned out squatters *had* been living in the basement, and they had left behind garbage and other less pleasant forms of waste.

"We'll have to get someone in here to clear this out," the cop said. "Unless you want to volunteer?"

I wasn't sure if he was joking. "No thanks." There was only so much I was willing to do for extra credit.

The cop waved everyone over. "No one is going in the building until the basement has been cleaned out. So everyone can go home." He seemed to direct that last part at the picketers.

"Well, this was a waste of time," I muttered to Matt and Charlie. And the picketers seemed way too happy with how this played out. It's not like they'd changed anything; the squatters were to blame for the delay.

Nina came back over toward me with her hands shoved in her jacket pockets. "So, I guess neither of us won this round."

"I guess not." She seemed to be waiting for me to continue the conversation. "I know you're waiting for me to say something, but I have no clue what you want to hear."

Matt and Charlie both cringed and walked away. Lisa chuckled and followed them.

"This sucks," Nina said.

"You'll have to be more specific."

"This…us…not talking."

I agreed with her but didn't know how to fix it. "I'd like to talk." Something crawled across my scalp. I grimaced and scratched my head. "I swear there are more spiders in my hair. I have to go."

All I wanted was a shower and food. The shower was the easy part. I washed my hair twice to make sure there weren't any more creepy crawlers hanging around.

I checked the refrigerator. Not much to choose from. I should have picked something up on the way home because hot dogs weren't going to cut it.

I could call for carryout, but did I want to bring food back here? It was Saturday night. Matt and Charlie had dates. They'd invited me to come along, but I didn't want to be a third wheel.

So, I walked out to my car with no clear plan. I heard laughter coming from Nina's backyard. What was she doing? Only one way to find out. I backtracked like I'd forgotten something, making sure to face her backyard.

Nina sat at a picnic table with her mom and brother. They were playing a board game. She glanced up at me with a question on her face. Decision time. I could ignore her or I could suck it up, admit I'd been a jerk, and see where that left us.

I walked over and said, "My hair is now arachnid free, so if you still want to talk we could go grab dinner."

"Okay, but first I need to ask you a question."

Jason's cell rang. He answered it and walked to the other side of the yard. Nina's mom stood up. "I'll go inside and give you guys a few minutes to hash this out."

Nina gestured at the recently vacated seat. I sat and waited to hear what she'd say.

"What was that about the other day?" She pointed toward the shed. "Did you kiss me because you wanted to kiss me or because you wanted to make a point?"

"Both." It was the truth.

"Okay." She leaned forward. "Then why did you abandon me?"

There was no answer to this question that wouldn't make me look like a dick. "Because sometimes I'm an overcompetitive jerk, and I was caught up in winning the argument?"

"Are you asking me or telling me?"

"Telling you, I guess. And I'm sorry." I reached across the table and laced my fingers through hers. "Does it help if I tell you that I've missed you and I know it was a dick move and I'll try to avoid doing anything like that again?"

"Yes, it does, and yes it was."

"I know. I'm sorry. So...are we good?" I asked.

"If we have problems in the future, do you promise you'll talk to me like a rational human being rather than running off and abandoning me? You know I have issues in that area."

Shit. I hadn't even thought about that. "I promise."

"All right then," she said. "Let's go grab dinner."

Thank goodness. Now we could go back to having fun together. I'd missed her, missed talking to her...heck, I even missed the way she liked to argue about everything.

Chapter Twenty-Seven

We ended up going to a barbecue place downtown. The food was good, and being around Nina felt right. After we left the restaurant, I had no idea what to do.

"Where to next?" I said. Because as long as I was with her, what we did really didn't matter. *Hell, did I just think that?* It seemed like one of those sappy greeting cards.

"It's such a nice night. Do you want to walk past the shops?"

God, no. Maybe I should have come up with a suggestion. Downtown was full of shops that sold antiques and little glass figurines that served no purpose on the planet except to collect dust.

"This is me being completely honest. I've never understood why people want to do that, but I'm willing to give it a shot. How about we walk past a few shops, and you can explain to me why it's supposed to be fun."

"Challenge accepted." She held out her hand. "The first rule of window shopping is that all couples strolling—"

"We're strolling? I'm not sure I've done that before. Do I need to stretch first?"

"Stroll, walk, wander, however you want to phrase it. The first rule of strolling past shops is you must hold hands."

"Okay." I held her hand. "Now what?"

"I'll explain as we go." She gestured toward the shops across the street. Once we'd made it to the first shop window, she said, "Second rule is, you look at whatever is in the window display and comment on it."

This particular shop sold antique dolls. A child-sized doll sat in a rocking chair in the window. It had realistic glass eyes that seemed to stare straight into your soul.

"So, what do you think?" Nina asked.

"I think that doll is terrifying and it would scar a child for life."

Nina laughed. "I agree. On to the next shop."

The next window featured blown-glass sculptures. "I love the blue and green vase," Nina said.

"I am resisting the impulse to mention dust."

"Thank you. If you weren't fixated on dust, which one would you buy?"

I studied my choices. They were works of art. One day, when I didn't live in a maze of Rubbermaid boxes, I might consider buying something like this. "I like the sunset-colored bowl."

"Good choice. That's my second favorite."

Apparently, I was getting the hang of this. More people had joined us on the sidewalk, and we shuffled along for a few minutes until we reached the next store. "Is there a rule for what you do between windows?" I asked.

"Nothing official. We can make small talk or people watch." She pointed toward a woman across the street wearing some sort of costume with wings on her back. "Whenever someone wears a costume like that in public I think it should be socially acceptable to ask them why. Is she in a play? Does she waitress at a fantasy bar?"

"A fantasy bar?"

"Yes. In my head there is a bar where people dress up like elves and fairies and whatever other fantasy creatures they want."

"I think that's called Comic-Con."

"Maybe." She pulled me toward the next window, which featured Christmas ornaments.

I hated Christmas. "How can a store that sells Christmas ornaments survive all year long?"

"I don't know," she said. "I'm not a big fan."

"Really? I imagined you'd have a tree decorated with book-themed ornaments."

"That would be pretty cool," she said. "But Christmas Day was when my mom figured out she wanted a divorce... So, not my favorite holiday."

"I'm not big on the holiday season either," I admitted.

"Any particular reason?" she asked.

She'd shared with me. I wanted to share some part of the truth with her. "My mom's condition flared up during the holidays a few years ago."

"Sorry." She squeezed my hand. "There should be a rule that bad stuff can't happen on holidays."

"That would be nice."

"I love the next store." She tugged me forward. In the window, there were paper sculptures made from books. It took me a moment to realize the books were open, and the paper had been cut or twisted to create scenes. "I'm surprised you're not offended on behalf of the books."

"I like that they've been turned into art." She pointed at one where the pages had been sculpted to look like a tree. "I love that one."

"I'm going to go with the obvious." I pointed at one that

said: READ.

"West? What are you doing here?"

I knew that voice. Keeping a calm expression on my face, I turned to see Vicky and Cole holding hands.

"According to Nina," I held up our joined hands, "I am strolling and window shopping."

Vicky smiled at Nina. "I have no idea how you got him to agree to this, but congratulations."

Nina shrugged. "I kind of sprung it on him. He's doing a pretty good job so far."

"Cole, help me out here. This is not a guy thing."

"No. It's a date thing. My take on it is, we're supposed to smile and nod and make mental notes for future birthday presents."

Vicky grinned. "In that case, there's the cutest jewelry store down the street." She tugged Cole in that direction.

Nina laughed. "Maybe it was fate that Vicky and Cole ended up together,"

"Whatever you say, Luna. On to the next window." She laughed, which is what I'd been going for. See, I could do this boyfriend thing. Maybe Vicky just hadn't been the right girl for me and, maybe, Nina was.

Chapter Twenty-Eight

NINA

I couldn't believe how well this evening was turning out. Part of me kept waiting for West to become annoyed about something, but so far so good. Once we reached the end of the block, we crossed the street and headed back toward the parking lot where we'd left his car. Holding West's hand felt right. I was waiting for him to let go. While I had a pretty firm grasp on window shopping, West and this whole dating thing was still a mystery.

When we got to the parking lot, he hit the unlock button on his key fob and the car lights flashed. I took that as my cue to release his hand. I opened the car door and climbed in. He walked around, got in, and started the car, but he didn't put his seat belt on. Instead, he leaned toward me. Like a dork, I already had my seat belt on. I leaned over while casually trying to hit the button to release the seat belt, but my fingers couldn't find the right spot.

West smiled at me. "Are you stuck?"

"Maybe." I glanced down at the seat belt release, which had twisted around and sunk into the seat. "*Uhm*...I think I might have to live in your car."

He laughed. "Allow me." He adjusted the seat belt back to its proper spot and hit the button.

"My hero," I said, before I leaned in and pressed my mouth against his, and then I stopped thinking. Everything narrowed down to his hand on my hip, pulling me toward him, and his mouth against mine. Despite the random bumps in our dating life so far, this part was easy. This part, being close to him like this...it worked. Too soon, he pulled away and drove out of the parking lot. I sat there in a happy post-kissing haze of bliss, feeling content with the world.

"Do you really want to go to the Valentine's Dance next weekend, or would you rather do something else? And please notice the hopeful tone in my voice about doing something else."

I laughed. "You're in luck, because in theory, school dances are supposed to be this magical experience. In reality, it's dressing up in uncomfortable clothes to stand around in the same place where a bunch of kids sweat every day. Doing something else sounds like a good plan to me."

"That's a relief," he said.

"I wonder what else is going on." I pulled out my cell and Googled local Valentine's events. "Some restaurants are offering special dinners, which probably means a limited menu where they charge twice the normal price."

West chuckled. "You're so cynical."

"I can't think of a single holiday that isn't stressful. I like Halloween because it's free license to eat as much chocolate as you want, but Thanksgiving and Christmas just make me feel stupid."

"Why?" he asked.

"Because I used to look forward to my dad coming home

for the holidays. My mom always made a big deal out of us being together as a family. She worked so hard to make everything perfect. And now, despite all that Hallmark-card-type bullshit, we're not together anymore. So the whole idea of the perfect family gathering seems like a big, fat lie."

"I used to like the holidays, back when my mom was nor—not sick."

The way he said it made me think he'd meant to say something else. We turned onto our street, and then he pulled in the driveway and parked.

"What were you going to say, before you said 'not sick?' And keep in mind that I've been baring my soul over here, so you don't have to worry about oversharing."

He turned the car off and stared at the steering wheel. "It sounds mean, and that's not how I want to sound. I was going to say back when she was normal."

I reached over and grabbed his hand. "I'm sorry. My dad made his choices, but your mom didn't choose to become ill." And now the mood had nose-dived. "On to happier topics." I scrolled through Valentine's Day events. "How would you feel about a chocolate festival? We'd buy tickets and sample some chocolate and watch pastry chefs create chocolate sculptures."

"Why don't we keep it simple and go to a movie?" he suggested.

"That will be plan B." The time on my cell said it was nine thirty. I was having so much fun, I didn't want the evening to end. "Do you want to come to my house and watch television?"

"Sure."

I unhooked my seat belt and then pointed at what I'd done. "Did you see?"

"Good job," he said, like he was praising a small child.

"Come on." I opened the car door and headed for my

front door. He fell into step beside me. The evening seemed surreal. Being with him made me happy. I think I made him happy, too. Wasn't that what you were supposed to look for? Someone who made you feel better when they were around, made you feel better about yourself? We may not be on the same side about keeping the library open, but as long as he was honest with me, everything would work out okay.

Chapter Twenty-Nine

I followed Nina to her front door. She'd been so honest with me. Could I tell her what was really going on with my mom? If my dad ever found out, he'd be furious. It's not like telling Nina would change the truth. Still…I hated not telling her the truth.

She unlocked the front door and Gidget bounded toward us. I could actually see dog fur flying off her as she moved.

"Hey, girl." Nina reached down to pet Gidget. More fur went flying. "Do you need to go outside?"

I followed Nina to the back patio doors. Gidget walked outside and trotted around the yard with her nose to the grass, sniffing so deeply I could see her ribs expand like bellows.

"Is she trying to inhale the grass?" I asked.

"She's probably on the trail of a rabbit," Nina said, "even though we have a no-eating-the-bunnies agreement, which she sticks to most of the time."

"What does that mean?"

"One day last spring, she brought my mom a bunny head,

as a gift."

"Just the head?"

Nina cringed. "Yes. Just the head. It was beyond disturbing. My mom and I both screeched and screamed and engaged in the mother of all freak-outs. So we traumatized the dog pretty good, too. Since then, we haven't had any incidents."

I now had two reasons not to have a dog: flying fur and random animal heads.

Wind whipped through the backyard. The temperature seemed to be dropping. It smelled like rain. I checked my cell. "Looks like a storm will be coming through."

"Fair warning, Gidget hates storms."

Lightning crackled off in the distance. Gidget's ears flattened to her head, and she dashed back inside.

We followed the dog and sat on the couch. Nina grabbed the remote and scanned through the channels. "What do you want to watch?"

"*American Ninja Warrior* is probably on."

"Sounds good." She found the right channel. One of the contestants was about to run up the warped wall. "I have no idea how they can do that."

"Practice," I said. "All the people who are really good built their own obstacle courses in their backyards or they belong to Ninja gyms."

"A Ninja gym sounds like fun," she said.

"You want to be a bookworm, hippie-chick, American Ninja?" The idea made me smile.

"Maybe."

Lightning flashed through the sky, followed by a blast of thunder that shook the house. Blonde fur streaked toward us and thumped into my chest. Suddenly, there was a large blonde beast on the couch with us.

"It's okay, Gidget." Nina hugged the dog who was sitting partially on her lap and part on mine. Gidget shivered and shoved her head under Nina's arm.

"What is she doing?"

"When she's scared, she turns into a giant lap dog."

Giant was right. She must weigh sixty pounds. "Is she trying to play ostrich?"

"I guess." Nina shrugged. "If my mom were home she'd be on her lap, instead."

Gidget pulled her head out and turned to look at me.

"You're kind of big to be a lap dog," I said, like she might understand what I was saying. She must've misinterpreted the message because she stood, turned in a circle, and jammed her head behind my shoulder, shoving me forward.

Nina laughed.

"Your dog is weird."

"Have you ever had a dog?" Nina asked.

"No, but Matt and Charlie do, and none of them ever acted like this."

Gidget pulled her head out, pressed it against my chest, and whined. Big brown soulful eyes stared up at me. I caved and petted her. She snuffled against my chest and then sighed. Something wound tight inside of me relaxed. Even though there was a giant dog sitting on my diaphragm, it felt like I could breathe a little easier.

"Behold the magic of dogs," Nina said in a quiet voice. "They unravel the stress in your soul."

I paused. "Did you read that on a pet store sign?"

"No, I found it on Pinterest," she said. "And I'd love to have it on a coffee mug because it's the absolute truth."

A jagged streak of lighting flashed through the sky followed by the crash of thunder. Gidget whined and looked at me like I was supposed to make the storm stop. "Sorry, I can't turn off the thunder."

"Hopefully, it will end soon," Nina said.

We watched people hold on to ledges with their fingertips

and run straight up walls for half an hour before the thunder stopped. Gidget finally relaxed enough to jump off the couch and go lie on her dog bed beside the coffee table. I was relieved, until I saw that half of Gidget's fur remained on my shirt and pants.

"Don't panic," Nina said. "We have fur rollers."

She scooted over, opened the drawer on the end table, and pulled out one of those sticky tape rollers.

"Do you have ten of those?"

"Probably. We buy them in bulk." She peeled the cover off and handed it over. "Give it a shot."

There was no way this thing would work, but it was my best option for the moment. I dragged the roller down the front of my shirt. In two swipes, it was full. I repeated the process and went through ten sticky sheets. "How is she not bald?"

"I ask her that question every day. And we asked the vet. Yellow Labs shed a lot."

"I think that's an understatement." Blonde strands of fur were still sprinkled across my shirt. I pulled at one piece. "It's like the fur imbeds in the fabric."

"It will come out in the dryer. Just be sure to empty your lint trap."

A disturbing image came to mind. "Your lint trap is full of dog fur, isn't it?"

"Yes."

And she wasn't the least bit upset by that fact. Just the idea of all my belongings covered in fur gave me the creeps. "You should distract me from the impending dog fur freak-out," I said.

"Maybe you should come this way a little bit." She reached over and put her hand on my shoulder and pulled me toward her. I met her halfway. Wrapping my arms around her and pulling her close felt natural. Everything about Nina felt soft and warm and right. Maybe there was something to her fate theory. Maybe we were meant to be together.

Chapter Thirty

We'd been kissing for a while when Gidget barked and ran to the front door. Reluctantly, I pulled away from West. "That must be my mom."

Sure enough, the door opened and my mom came in. Gidget did her happy homecoming dance.

"Hey, Mom."

"Hello, dear. Hello, West. How'd Gidget do with the storm?"

West snorted.

"She sat on both of our laps," I said.

"There are more lint rollers in the pantry, West, if you need them."

West brushed at the front of his shirt, which was still sprinkled with blonde fur. "I was thinking more along the lines of a Shop-Vac."

My mom smiled. "It's a small price to pay for all this love." She ruffled Gidget's ears. "Come in the kitchen with me, girl. I bought more chewies."

Gidget trailed after my mom into the kitchen. West scooted forward to the edge of the couch cushion like he planned to stand.

"I should go," he said.

"Okay. I had fun tonight."

"Me, too." He stood and held out his hand. "Walk me to the back door."

Living next door to the person you were dating made saying good-bye interesting. I let West pull me to my feet, and we walked to the patio door. I peered outside. "The rain isn't too bad."

"And it's not like I have far to go," he said.

Part of me wanted to ask him if we were officially dating…like a couple. He'd window-shopped with me, and we'd discussed plans for our anti-Valentine's Day weekend, so did that indicate we were a couple? What if the question freaked him out?

He glanced toward the kitchen where my mom had gone. Her being home must have spooked him because he barely brushed his lips across mine before pulling away. "Good night, Nina."

"Good night." I opened the glass sliding doors, and he darted out and across the yards to his own back door. I watched until he went inside. When I turned back around, my mom was sitting on the couch next to Gidget who was gnawing on a rawhide bone.

"Did I chase him off?"

I shut and locked the door. "I think it was a combination of dog fur and you coming home."

"Sorry."

I crossed the room and sat down beside her. "No big deal. We had a great night." I recapped the dinner and our window shopping experience.

"It sounds like he's making an effort," my mom said. "That's a good sign."

"I thought so, too." The fact that he thought I was worth making an effort for gave me a warm fuzzy.

• • •

Sunday afternoon I went shopping with Lisa. It was stock-up day at her house. She hit Target, while her mom did the grocery shopping. They called it the divide-and-conquer technique.

My mom or I shopped randomly throughout the week, whenever we needed food or toilet paper, which worked for us.

"I don't know where you have room to store all this stuff." I helped her wrestle a twenty-four pack of toilet paper onto the bottom of the cart.

"There're two of us in a three-bedroom house, so the third room is like a giant storage closet." Lisa pushed the cart down the aisle. After we finished buying enough paper products and laundry detergent to last a month, we went to a teahouse for lunch.

"So, now that I'm dating West instead of not-not dating West, do you want me to ask him about Matt?"

Lisa stirred sugar into her tea. "Matt is cute, and he seems like a good guy. I had fun talking to him at Bixby's, but I think if he were interested, he would have asked me out already. I get the feeling he's waiting on someone who isn't available."

"Why do you say that?"

"He mentioned his sister's best friend Jane more than once. And his face kind of lit up when he talked about her."

"That's too bad."

"No big deal. Like I said before, I'm enjoying a drama-free period right now."

"I can't remember a time when my life was drama free," I said. "Though lately, at least, it's been good drama."

After lunch, we drove by the Hilmer Library, which now sported a sign that read: HILMER RECYCLING CENTER COMING SOON.

"I guess a recycling center isn't a bad thing," she said.

"It's useful, but it's not magical like a library."

"It keeps stuff out of landfills, which is kind of magical," she said. "But nothing is as magical as a library or a bookstore."

Chapter Thirty-One

Sunday afternoon, while my mother sat reading in her room and my father went grocery shopping, I snuck into the living room to empty out some boxes. I climbed into the small area I'd cleared in the middle and opened one of the unmarked containers. My dad hadn't started using a Sharpie on everything until the furniture was covered, so I had no idea what I'd find, which was slightly frightening.

Inside the container, I found cardboard tubes from rolls of paper towels and a small wooden chest. That was odd. Why put a box in a box? I opened the chest to see doll clothes, which was weird since no one in this house had ever played with dolls. Must be something my mom had picked up at a garage sale. I shoved the cardboard tubes in one bag and the clothes in another. Since the clothes looked brand new, I'd drop them off at Goodwill.

"West, what are you doing?"

I froze. How had my father crept up on me like that?

"What does it look like I'm doing?"

"It looks like you're trying to bail out a sinking ship with a teaspoon." He chuckled like it was a joke. I didn't think it was funny.

"I have to try." I met his gaze. "One of us has to try. She doesn't even know what's in these tubs. So why keep this crap?"

"It's not her fault," he said.

"I understand, but we shouldn't have to live like this." I pointed toward the area where I thought the couch still was. "We should be able to sit in the living room, like normal people."

"You won't live here forever," he said. "You'll go away to college, and then you'll have your own house. Live your own life. In the meantime, don't upset the balance of your mom's life…and mine."

We'd never talked about college. "True, but I haven't heard back from any of the scholarships I applied for, so I don't even know if I can go to school."

He blinked at me like he didn't understand what I'd said. "We never talked about this, but I thought you knew."

"Knew what?"

"You have a college fund. We started it when you were born. It won't pay for Ivy League, but it will get you through a state school."

I was caught somewhere between relieved and angry. "Why didn't you tell me?"

He waved his hands at all the boxes. "I was a little preoccupied."

"Right." I could be mad, or I could accept this as the gift it was. I slumped back against a stack of boxes. "Thank you. You have no idea what a relief that is."

"You need to put those back." My dad pointed at the frilly dresses.

"Why would she want doll clothes?"

"Those aren't for dolls," he said with a catch in his voice. "Those were meant for your sister."

The room seemed to shift around me. "Sister?"

He rubbed the back of his neck and looked down at the floor. "You were too young to realize what was going on at the time, but your mom...she miscarried when you were two years old. We tried again after that, but things didn't go as planned. We could have gone to specialists, but your mom refused. She said if it was meant to be, it would happen."

This was way out of my league. I had no idea what to say except, "I'm sorry."

He nodded. "Me, too. Anyway, I'm making spaghetti. Why don't you put all of that back and help with the salad."

The dresses I folded and put neatly back in the wooden chest before replacing them in the box, but the bag of cardboard tubes I kept out. "I'm going to put these in the recycling bin."

"It's not worth upsetting your mother," he said. "Just put it all back."

I needed to tread lightly. "I have a recurring nightmare that while I'm sleeping, the house sinks into the ground because there's so much junk in it. And I'm trapped...we're all trapped underground with all this garbage...and we can't escape."

"You will escape," he said. "Put those back and come help with dinner."

Feeling defeated, I shoved the cardboard back in the storage box and snapped the lid shut.

Once dinner was on the table, I hollered for my mother because there were times I couldn't face seeing her perched on her bed amid the chaos. In the kitchen, she looked sort of normal, or I could pretend she did.

She joined us, smiling a normal-person smile. I'd take that for now.

I ate my spaghetti while I thought about the news my dad had given me. I didn't have to win a scholarship. There was money to get me out of this house. The relief I felt at the thought of escaping this place made me feel guilty.

When my dad smiled and talked to my mom, he looked at her the same way he'd always looked at her—with love. Could my mom see the frustration on my face when I spoke to her? I hoped not. Maybe I should work on that—just accepting her as she was.

"How are things with Nina?" she asked, pulling me from my thoughts.

I smiled. "Things are pretty good."

"She has such a cute dog," my mom said. "I've seen them playing Frisbee."

"That's Gidget." I told my mom about how the dog was afraid of thunder.

"They sound like a nice family," my mom said.

My dad was quiet.

"Does it still bother you that I'm seeing Nina?" I asked.

"As long as she doesn't hit your car again, I'm okay with it," he said.

• • •

Monday morning I sat in my car and waited for Nina to join me. She seemed to constantly run ten minutes late, no matter what we were doing. I'd finished my most recent book, so I was Googling ideas for anti-Valentine's Day, which was coming up this Friday.

Apparently, there were a lot of angry women in the world

because there were multiple suggestions on how to make voodoo dolls of your ex and suggestions for picture-burning parties. Funny, but this weekend, I'd realized how much my dad still loved my mom. It made me want to try harder to help him. Not that I wasn't counting down the days until I could go away to school, but while I was here, I'd make more of an effort to be sympathetic.

The car door opened, and Nina smiled at me as she climbed in. "You look happy this morning."

"Don't I normally look happy?"

"No." She set her bag on the floor and put on her seat belt. "You always look like you're brooding or focusing on something, like you're trying to solve a problem."

Huh. Do other people see me that way? "Maybe I don't look that way today because one of my problems has been solved. My dad and I talked about college and apparently, I have a college fund he never mentioned."

Nina's mouth dropped open for a second. "Why didn't he tell you about that so you wouldn't stress about scholarships?"

"I think he thought I knew. And at first I was mad about not knowing, but now I'm just happy the money is there."

"I'm so happy for you," she said. "Do you know where you want to go?"

I wanted to escape, but suddenly and surprisingly, I also felt the need to be close, in case my dad needed me. "I'm still not sure."

Chapter Thirty-Two

I was happy for West, but the idea of him moving away made my stomach hurt a little. Our relationship, whatever it was we had, probably wouldn't end up as a happily ever after, because that only happened in fairy tales. Knowing for sure he was going to run away as soon as possible wasn't something I wanted to think about. But worrying too much about the future would only destroy what we had now. I was back to my "Be more like the dog" mantra. I needed to live in the moment and take things as they came.

On that note, I said, "Valentine's Day is this Friday."

"And all those times I said we weren't going to the dance, I was right," he gloated. "Because we're going to the movies, instead."

"Okay, technically you're right, but we're still actually doing something together on Valentine's Day, which I think is what you were objecting to in the first place, so I think I'm right, too."

"You have to argue about everything," he said, "don't you?"

If he'd said it in an angry tone, I would have been upset, but he was smiling so I knew he was teasing me.

"It's not arguing." I moved toward him. "It's debating. And it's fun."

"It is?" He leaned toward me.

"Yes." I closed the distance between us and kissed him. He kissed me back. Unfortunately, we had to go, so I ended the kiss and put on my seat belt.

West pulled out of the driveway and headed toward school.

"Back to Valentine's Day," I said. "Maybe we could go to the chocolate exhibition and then go to the movies. Because even though I'm anti-Valentine's Day, I am pro-chocolate."

"They sell chocolate at the movie theater. You can buy a three-pound candy bar and eat the entire thing, if you want."

That didn't work for me. "I could, but it wouldn't be fancy chocolate."

"What's that mean?"

"Giftable chocolate."

"Giftable?" he asked.

"Chocolate in a pretty box," I explained, "for a special occasion." Which also meant they were for a special person.

"So we could go to the show, buy chocolate, and I could stick a bow on it," he said.

"Not the same."

"Chocolate is chocolate."

"You could be stuck with a girlfriend who demanded flowers and jewelry for Valentine's Day," I said, "so you're getting off easy."

West didn't respond. He just turned on the radio. I decided not to push the issue because it wasn't worth debating at the moment. Once we made it to school and parked, he gave me a strange look.

"What's wrong?" I asked.

"Nothing." He turned the car off and reached for his door handle.

What could I have said that would have flipped the switch on his mood from happy to crabby? And that's when it hit me. "Are you freaking out because I used the word *girlfriend*?"

He wouldn't meet my gaze.

"Oh my God. Seriously?"

"It's stupid," he said. "Just forget about it."

Like that was going to happen. "Me thinking of myself as your girlfriend is stupid, or are you referring to the fact that you're freaking out?" I needed some clarification before *I* became crabby.

He reached up and rubbed the back of his neck. "That's a loaded question. Any answer I give will tick you off. Let's forget about it. Okay?"

A cold rush of self-doubt filled my stomach, making me nauseous. We'd been having fun until I implied we were in a real relationship. We were in a relationship, weren't we? "West, this is important. I need to know I'm not just convenient."

"What are you talking about?" Now he sounded frustrated.

This was not how I wanted to spend my morning. I closed my eyes and rubbed my temples. How could I say what I wanted to say without sounding needy? I didn't want to sound needy.

I heard the car door open and shut and then the sound of footsteps moving across the gravel lot. Had he ditched me again? Seriously?

My car door swung open. West stood there holding out his hand. "Come here."

"Why?"

"I'm trying to fix this, and you're making it difficult. Get out of the damn car."

A smooth talker he was not. Still, I was curious about what he would say. I unbuckled my seat belt and grabbed my bag before taking his hand.

He pulled me from the car. "I'm pretty sure this whole boyfriend-girlfriend relationship thing, which apparently I'm bad at, is like window shopping." He pointed at our joined hands. "We hold hands and walk through the parking lot, which shows anyone in the immediate vicinity, including you, that you're not convenient."

"Thank you for clearing that up."

"I'd never call you convenient…you're actually more of a pain in the ass."

"Ha. Ha." I poked him in the chest.

"You know I'm mostly kidding." He leaned in and kissed me. When he pulled away, he said, "From now on, I'd like advance notice before you use scary words. That way, we can avoid my momentary freak-outs and your meltdowns."

"I can't think of any other scary relationship words that might come up in the near future," I said. "But if I do, I'll let you know."

"Okay. Let's rewind this conversation back to the part where we're going to the show and I'm being emotionally blackmailed into buying you fancy chocolate."

"That totally works for me." Crisis averted.

"Of course it does. Let's go."

We walked across the parking lot holding hands, and people did seem to notice. I smiled at anyone who checked us out.

For the rest of the week, I did my best not to be overly sensitive to anything West said, because I was beginning to learn that while males and females shared the same language, the things they said didn't always mean the same thing.

Plus, he liked me and was making an effort to avoid things that would freak me out, so I decided to do the same. Friday morning, when I climbed into the car there was a giant, red, heart-shaped box of candy taking up most of my seat.

"Happy Valentine's Day." West gestured at the giant heart box as if I might miss it.

"Thank you." It might be corny, and the presentation wasn't awesome, but my heart still skipped a beat. "Happy Valentine's Day to you, too." I picked up the box, climbed in, and leaned over to kiss him.

When the kiss ended, I said, "I have something for you." I pulled the card I'd bought him from my backpack. He opened the red envelope and laughed at the Teenage Mutant Ninja Turtle card inside and smiled when he opened it and saw the Amazon gift card.

"I almost bought you a gift card to the bookstore, but I knew you preferred ebooks."

"Thank you."

On the drive to school, I ate two caramel-filled chocolates. "Do you want one?"

"No thanks."

I closed the lid of the heart-shaped box. Too bad it wouldn't fit in my locker. Then I'd be able to stop for chocolate breaks between classes.

When we pulled into the school parking lot, I laughed. Red and pink balloons were tied to several cars' windshield wipers. One car was covered in hot pink hearts that looked like they were made with silly string.

"Why?" West said, as he gestured at the oddly decorated cars.

"I'm not sure. You'd think people would put the balloons

on their boyfriends' or girlfriends' car when it was in their driveway because the person receiving the balloons won't see them until after school."

"I'm glad you liked the chocolates, but holidays are still stupid," West said.

"Agreed." We walked through the parking lot holding hands. No one seemed to pay much attention because we weren't a brand-new couple anymore. I kissed him good-bye at his locker and went on to my locker to meet Lisa. She did not look like a happy camper.

"Good morning," I said. "If you need to vent about the stupidity of the holiday, I'm here to listen."

She frowned. "I'm glad things worked out for you and West, but it sucks being the odd man out. I might feel better if there was anyone I even liked, but the only guy I'm interested in has friend-zoned me."

"You mean Matt?" I asked.

"Yeah, I said hi to him this morning, and he looked like he wanted to bolt, like I was going to throw myself at him because it was Valentine's Day."

"Sorry."

A girl down the hall squealed about something—probably cheap flowers or some other Valentine's gift. "That's happened twice since I've been here," she said. "And it's freaking annoying."

"One of my goals in life," I said, "is to never make that girly, high-pitched squealing noise."

"Agreed," Lisa said. "It's undignified."

Apparently, the rest of the female population of Greenbrier High didn't feel that way because random outbursts happened throughout the day. If I didn't have West, I would've been more annoyed. This was my first successful Valentine's Day so far in life.

. . .

After the drive home from school, West said, "So what movie did you want to see?"

He pulled up the movie times on his cell. "Your choices are a spy thriller or a buddy comedy."

"There are ten movies showing. And I'm pretty sure they have titles."

He grinned. "I said I'd take you to the movies. I didn't say I planned on watching the show."

I laughed. "We're watching some of it." I snatched the phone from his hand and scrolled down the choices. "Comedy at seven forty-five works for me." I handed back his phone.

Several hours later, I was using a sticky tape roller to remove Gidget fur from my black sweater. I checked the results in the mirror. Random pieces of fur still stuck out at odd angles. I tried the roller again and then gave up. I loved Gidget, but from now on maybe I should buy only cream-colored clothes.

I went downstairs and saw my mom frowning at a heart-shaped vase full of yellow daisies. There was only one person who would have sent her those—my dad.

"So...those are a surprise," I said.

"Yes. They are. I'm caught between wanting to throw them in the trash and not wanting to waste pretty flowers just because an idiot sent them to me."

"My vote would be to put them down the garbage disposal one at a time."

My mom gave a bitter laugh. "I don't understand what he thinks he's doing. There's not a chance in hell I will ever forgive him. He has to know that."

There was a small card attached to the vase. "What does the card say?"

"Some crap about how I'm his one true love." My mom's

voice broke. She sniffled. "Ugh…I hate that he can still make me so mad I cry."

I told her about West's toxic skunk theory, which made her laugh.

"I knew I liked that boy." She sighed and then grabbed the vase. "Would you get the front door for me?"

"Sure." What was she planning on doing?

First she dumped the water from the vase, and then she walked out onto the front porch and swung the vase like a pail of water, launching the daisies across the lawn.

"If I know your father, he's planning on driving by to see if he can talk to me. This should send him a pretty clear signal that he should keep on driving."

West approached in my peripheral vision. "Should I ask?"

"Toxic skunk flowers," my mom said. "Have a fun night." And then she turned back around and went into the house.

"Okay then," West said. "Time for our anti-Valentine's Day movie."

It turned out that the movie wasn't very good. Not that we watched a lot of it. West kept distracting me…in a good way. We kissed our way through most of the movie and once the lights came up, my brain was fairly scrambled.

The cool evening air helped restore my faculties as we walked to the car. "Where to now?" I asked.

"We have two choices. Matt and Charlie are having a bonfire, or we can hang out at your place."

"I'm not in the mood to be around a bunch of people." I was pretty sure he was thinking about sneaking out to the shed so we could be alone, but I wasn't about to suggest that.

When we pulled into the driveway, he said, "Did I mention that I restocked the shed with s'mores Pop-Tarts?"

"I've never tried that flavor." And that was the truth, but it wasn't the Pop-Tarts I was really interested in.

We snuck back to the shed, and I laughed when I saw what West had done. There was a box of s'mores Pop-Tarts on top of the mini-fridge and another much smaller heart-shaped box of chocolates on the love seat.

"Very nice," I said.

He smiled. "I might be getting the hang of this whole boyfriend thing."

I pretended to be shocked, placing my hand over my heart. "You said the *B* word."

"I did." He pulled me close. "And you should probably distract me before I freak out."

I played with the hair at the nape of his neck and smiled up at him. "I can do that."

A tiny voice in my brain whispered that this was too good to be true. I ignored that annoying voice in favor of kissing West.

Chapter Thirty-Three

Saturday morning, my dad made French toast, which was my mom's favorite breakfast. He hummed as he cooked, and I did my best not to think about why he seemed so happy this morning. There are some places your mind shouldn't go.

I opted for grabbing a packet of Pop-Tarts and heading back to my room to read a book because that made living in denial a little easier.

I'd been reading for about an hour when a text from Nina popped up on my cell. *Are you busy? My mom cooks when she's annoyed. We have enough hash brown casserole and banana bread to feed the entire block.*

Sounded good to me. The Pop-Tarts I'd eaten were long gone. I texted back that I'd be right over.

Nina greeted me at the front door with a smile and a quick kiss. She whispered, "Don't mention Valentine's Day, or my dad."

I nodded to show I understood.

Gidget trotted over and looked at me expectantly. I reached down to pet her head. She leaned into me and dog fur drifted through the air. "This can't be normal."

"It's normal for her," Nina said. "Watch this. Gidget, do you want hash browns?"

The dog proceeded to stamp her front feet, dancing around like a toddler on Red Bull.

"Again," I pointed at Gidget. "Not normal."

Nina laughed. I followed her into the kitchen. "Help yourself," Nina said. "While I take care of my furry beast."

Jason was already seated at the table. He nodded at me and then went back to shoveling food into his mouth. The savory scent of cheese and bacon made my mouth water. I grabbed a plate and scooped out a large helping of what looked like hash browns mixed with eggs, cheese, and bacon. That couldn't be bad.

Nina dropped a small glob of hash browns in Gidget's bowl. The dog wolfed it down in five seconds and then came to stare at me with the intensity of the sun as I took every bite. "Is that really necessary?" I asked Gidget. Her tail swooped back and forth.

"She's already had some of mine and some of Nina's," Jason said. "So you're the next logical target."

"Can't blame her," I said. "These are amazing."

"Thank you," Nina's mom said from the stove where she stirred something in a pan.

I ate two helpings and then leaned back in my seat. "I need a nap."

Jason yawned. "I believe that's next on my agenda." He put his plate in the sink and then headed toward the stairs.

Nina grabbed our plates and put them both in the sink. "Let's go sit on the couch and try not to fall asleep."

"Okay."

Nina turned the television on and then whispered,

"Apparently, my dad didn't interpret the flowers strewn across the front yard correctly. He thought it meant please come to the door and plead your sorry-ass case. My mom refused to even open the door because he might've thought that meant he was welcome to come inside, which he totally is not."

"Not to be rude, but is he stupid or delusional?" I asked. "Because I can't think of a person alive who'd forgive that kind of betrayal."

"You have no idea how relieved I am that you understand."

We watched television for a while as her mom banged pots and pans around in the kitchen. After yawning for the third time, I said. "That's it. We're going for a walk or something because if we keep sitting here I'm going to fall into a carbohydrate and fat-induced coma."

"I know exactly what you mean." She stood and we headed out the front door. When we hit the end of the driveway, Nina reached for my hand. It felt natural to lace my fingers through hers, which was kind of frightening. That was another one of those things it was probably better not to think about.

A breeze lifted her hair and sent it flying around her face. She released my hand and pulled a band from her wrist, which she used to put her hair in a ponytail.

"Are you always armed with ponytail holders?" I asked as she slid her hand back into mine and we continued down the street.

"Yes. You can normally count on me to have ponytail holders, a book, and a fair amount of dog fur," she said. "What are you always carrying?"

"My keys and my cell." I thought about it. "That's about it, unless I've spent time at your house." I pointed at my right pant leg, which had a disturbing amount of dog fur on it. "Gidget leaned against me for like ten seconds. I don't understand how this is possible."

Nina grinned. "She's a giver."

We walked around the block, making small talk. It was comfortable. By the time we made it back to our driveway, I was awake. Going back to Nina's house didn't sound like a great plan. Of course we couldn't go to my house, which left the BBQ court or the shed. I knew which one I'd pick. "Where to now?" I asked.

Her cell buzzed. She checked the text and frowned. "Crap. I forgot that I told Lisa we'd hang out today. What's up with Matt, anyway?"

"Those are two separate topics," I said. "What time are you supposed to meet Lisa?"

"In an hour," she said. "Now what's up with your cousin?"

"I have no idea." And that was the truth. I wasn't going to repeat what Charlie had said about Matt being into someone who wasn't available because that could cause all sorts of problems, especially if Nina figured out who it was.

"Not helpful," she said. She texted Lisa back and then said. "I better go help my mom clean up the kitchen before I meet Lisa. You're welcome to join me for dish duty if you like."

"No, thank you. I have books to read." I walked her to her door and kissed her good-bye. "See you later."

• • •

NINA

I met Lisa at the bookstore so she could pick out a new book boyfriend. We both found a few books that sounded interesting, and then we browsed the adult coloring book section.

Lisa showed me a coloring book with butterflies. "This one looks cool."

"I like the ones with geometric patterns better." I flipped through a few and found what I was looking for. I held it out to Lisa. "See, I can color these however I want."

"I'm getting the butterflies. They seem so optimistic."

We browsed the clearance area. "Hey, look. Sparkly gel pens are on sale." I waved the package at Lisa.

"Didn't you buy a package of those last weekend?" she asked.

"You can never have too many sparkly gel pens." At least that was my theory. "And they're 60 percent off, so your argument is invalid."

Lisa rolled her eyes. "Fine."

After paying for our treasures, we headed back to the cafe for caramel lattes.

My cell beeped with a text. I read it and grinned. "Guess who needs to design a poster for the Keep the Hilmer Library Open campaign?"

"I'm going to go with *us*," Lisa said.

"You are correct, because the library ladies managed to get us permission to hang posters all over the school and around town. We even have a small budget to make copies."

As we drank our coffees, Lisa and I worked at coming up with slogans for the campaign.

"Nothing too cutesy," I said. "Because we want guys to agree with us, too."

"So I guess, *Keep the library open because book boyfriends are better than real boys* isn't an option," Lisa said.

I laughed. "Probably not." I took a sip of my latte. "What about, *Save the bookworm's natural habitat?*"

"I'm not sure everyone would understand what that meant," Lisa said. "Maybe we should keep it simple."

After tossing out and shooting down a dozen more ideas, we settled on, *Keep the Hilmer Library Open. Recycle a Different Building.*

"It's not super imaginative, but it gets the message across loud and clear," I said.

"We should go pick up some copies of the official petition and ask students to sign it to show their support," Lisa said. "Let's go back to my house to work on this. We don't want West to know what we're up to."

"Good idea." West probably wouldn't be thrilled, but I think he understood now that this wasn't an attack on him. I just had a different opinion, which I was entitled to. I was never going to be one of those girls who agreed with everything a guy said. And if I was going to be a grown-up about it, I had to admit that he was entitled to his opinion, too.

After we created the poster and had copies made, we had one more problem. "When are we going to hang these?" I asked.

"I bet we could get into the building super early tomorrow," Lisa said. "And hang them before anyone else comes in."

I groaned. "I hate super early. It's a terrible time to go anywhere."

"It's for the library," Lisa reminded me. "And bragging rights after we beat West."

"Since it's for the library, I'll tell West I'm helping you with something so I won't need a ride to school tomorrow." Would he be willing to give me a ride home from school once he saw the posters? That was another question.

Lisa picked me up psycho-early the next morning. We spent an hour taping posters onto every flat surface in the school building. When we were down to half a dozen, I checked my cell. West should be showing up soon. And I knew just how I wanted to greet him.

Chapter Thirty-Four

Driving to school Monday morning, I couldn't help thinking Nina was up to something. The way she had evaded answering my questions when I asked why she was riding to school with Lisa was a dead giveaway.

As soon as I stepped foot into the building I was smacked in the face by the neon orange posters lining the hallways that said: KEEP THE HILMER LIBRARY OPEN. RECYCLE A DIFFERENT BUILDING.

Even if I hadn't caught Nina in the act of taping one of the posters above my locker, I would have guessed she was behind this.

"Don't even think about it," I said. "Or that sign is going to become a paper airplane."

Nina turned around and grinned at me like she was quite satisfied with herself. "Come on. It's a little funny."

"It's not," I said. "Unless you want pro-recycling bumper stickers in an equally ugly neon color plastered all over your

Jeep, go post your sign somewhere else."

"I have several responses to that. First off, these signs are not ugly. They're a bright happy shade of orange meant to catch people's eyes."

"Or blind them," I said.

She stuck her tongue out at me. "Second, it's not like I'm anti-recycling. And thirdly—"

"Third-ly? Is that even a real word?"

She laughed. "If it wasn't before, it is now. So…thirdly, if you put bumper stickers on my Jeep, I'll put Hello Kitty stickers all over your car."

"Hello Kitty?" I had a hard time pretending to be annoyed because she seemed to be having such a good time stating her case. "What does a glittery cat have to do with the library versus recycling center argument?"

"Not much, but I bought a bunch on clearance at the bookstore so they're my go-to revenge stickers of the moment. And we're not arguing." She smiled and moved closer. "We're debating." She pulled on the strap of my backpack so I'd lean forward. "It's fun." And then she kissed me. My brain pointed out that Nina was a strange girl who got turned on by arguing. My body didn't care. I snaked an arm around her waist and pulled her close.

There were catcalls and some laughter. She pulled away from me and said, "See, this is fun."

"I still don't understand your form of crazy," I said. "But it's working for me."

Nina chuckled and continued down the hall toward her locker. Matt and Charlie stood off to the side, with judgmental looks on their faces. "What?"

"She distracted you." Charlie pointed at the shiny new poster that hung above my locker. The one I'd sort of forgotten about when she'd kissed me.

I might have walked away and left it up there. "Sneaky,

argumentative, hippy chick," I muttered under my breath as I tore the poster down.

I planned on talking to Mr. Grant about the whole library project in social studies. I hadn't planned on him bringing it up to the entire class.

"Students, even though it's Monday, I'm sure you noticed the posters in the hallway this morning. There's a group of concerned students and citizens who don't want Hilmer Library closed until the new library is built."

There went my extra credit.

"Some of you may have heard there were squatters in the basement of the building. My brother-in-law sent some men in to clean the basement out. Instead of going ahead with the plan to rehab the building as soon as possible, we've decided to let each group make its case and then whoever wants to can sign a petition so that you all can see democracy in action on a personal level."

Nina probably loved this. "Not to be selfish, but how will this affect our extra credit?"

"I'm assuming you're still pro-recycling center?" he said.

"Yes."

"Then you can choose to create posters and hang them up or hand out fliers."

"I just wanted to hit something with a sledgehammer," I said, only sort of joking.

Mr. Grant laughed. "You may still get your chance. In the meantime, you can meet with other students and develop a campaign strategy."

This was not what I had signed up for.

"You might be interested to know that the recycling company has several posters about the benefits of recycling on their website, which you can print out."

That didn't sound so bad. "So I should print those out and give them to other students to hand out or hang up?" Delegating, I could do.

"Yes, and keep a journal of your efforts. When the dust settles I'll give you credit on your effort, not on whether your side wins or not."

Good to know, but I was going to win. I just needed to come up with a strategy. Toward the end of class Mr. Grant let me use one of the classroom computers. I pulled up the recycling center and printed out some educational posters. Then I scanned the site for any free promotional swag they might hand out. They offered combs. That was boring. Key tags. Yawn.

Mr. Grant came over to check on me. "What are you looking for?"

"I hoped to find some sort of giveaway that would get students to sign our petition."

"You can try," he said. "But I don't think you'll find anything from the recycling centers for free that students will care about."

He was right. What would make students sign a petition? "Could we do a raffle? If you sign the petition, your name is entered for some sort of prize?"

"You could, but we don't have a budget. Maybe a local restaurant would donate a gift certificate if you put their logo on your poster."

This was becoming too complicated. "Do you know anyone who might help out?"

"Let's ask the class." He announced the plan and asked the question.

A girl raised her hand. "My aunt opened a new pizza restaurant downtown. She'd probably donate a meal for the free advertising."

And now I had a plan.

After school, I found Nina waiting in the parking lot by my car. She smiled at me but didn't look quite sure of herself. "So can I text Lisa that you're giving me a ride home?"

"Are you armed with Hello Kitty stickers?" I asked.

"Nope."

I clicked my key fob. "Then you can get in the car."

She climbed in. As I drove home, she said, "So I heard a rumor you're offering a pizza raffle to anyone who signs your petition."

"I can neither confirm nor deny that statement." And really I couldn't because the girl hadn't talked to her aunt yet.

"The library ladies already have a petition," she said. "I guess whatever signatures we gather will be added to theirs."

"Sounds like a gang for grandmothers," I said. "Beware the library ladies."

. . .

NINA

"Never underestimate the power of a reader, no matter how old they are. I bet those ladies are tied into all sorts of restaurants and stores in town. Maybe I could ask one of them to donate a raffle prize."

"You're going to try to out-raffle me, aren't you?" West asked.

"Now that you mention it." I laughed, but I didn't want this to become awkward. "How about we make a promise that no matter what happens with the library, we won't get mad at each other."

"I'll get extra credit based on my efforts, no matter what ends up happening, so I can agree to that. I'd like to point out that you're the one with a temper."

I laughed. "I'm not the only one with a temper."

"Let me rephrase that," he said. "You're extremely argumentative."

"I can't argue with that." I poked him in the shoulder. "See what I did there?"

He snorted but didn't comment. Things seemed comfortable between us, which was nice. I guess we'd wait and see what the future would bring. It was weird now that Valentine's Day was over. For so long that date had been something we were working toward. Now I guess we were taking things day by day.

"Want to come over for some dog fur and banana bread?" I asked when he parked in the driveway.

A look of horror crossed his face. "There isn't any dog fur in the banana bread…right?"

I made no promises. "Of course not. Unless a piece drifted into the batter."

"I may never eat at your house again." The look of revulsion on his face made it hard not to laugh.

"You've already eaten at my house several times, so even if there is the occasional stray piece of dog fur in your food, it hasn't killed you yet."

"I'm going to pretend we never had this conversation, because your mom is a good cook and home-cooked meals are a rarity at my house." West climbed out of the car and walked toward my front door.

I followed after him, thinking he needed a hug and how sad it was that no one cooked for him.

After West left to meet up with his cousins, I took Gidget out into the backyard to throw the Frisbee. The light was on in the kitchen at his house, so I snuck a glance. A woman, who I assumed was West's mom, looked out the window. Maybe if I didn't make direct eye contact I wouldn't scare her off.

When Gidget was panting like crazy, I stopped throwing and checked the window. West's mom smiled and gave a small wave. *Progress.* I returned her greeting and she gestured that I should come closer. That was unexpected.

Moving slowly so I wouldn't scare her off, I walked across the yard toward the window. West's mom didn't look sick, but she did look a little nervous and lost, kind of like someone who walked into a party but wasn't sure they'd been invited.

When I was a few feet from the window, I said, "Hello, I'm Nina. You must be West's mom."

"I am. It's nice to meet you." She pointed at Gidget. "Your dog is so pretty."

"Thank you." I reached down to pet her head. "She's a good girl."

"Can I pet her?" she asked.

"Sure." A little voice in my head wondered if this was a good idea. His mom would know better than to do anything to risk her own health, right?

"Bring her to the back door," his mom said and then she disappeared from view.

I walked Gidget to the patio door. Was this okay? Should I text West?

His mom pulled back the curtain, which normally blocked the view through the patio doors. She stood there on the other side of the sliding glass door with an uncertain look on her face. She placed her hand on the door handle and then drew it back, hesitating. Through the glass door I could see what wasn't visible from the kitchen window. Her pink robe was frayed at the edges. The pajamas she wore underneath appeared clean, but she had on two different slippers. Weird.

Slowly, she slid the door open and held her hand out toward Gidget. "Hello, girl."

Gidget sniffed West's mom's hand and then leaned into

her touch. Very gently, his mom ran her hand over Gidget's head and ears. Blonde fur drifted through the air.

"She sheds a lot," I said.

"Oh my. Yes, she does," West's mom said. "But I don't mind."

"West is such a neat freak," I said. "It really bothered him at first."

"He gets that from his father." She squatted down to pet Gidget, and I saw past her into the kitchen, which was normal. What wasn't normal was the stack of Rubbermaid boxes I could see in the living room. And not just a few boxes. The small slice of living room I could see was nothing but boxes stacked one on top of another.

It felt like cold marbles were rolling around in my stomach. "Are you moving?"

"No." She stood. "Why do you ask?"

"The boxes," I said. "I thought maybe you were packing."

"No." She smiled. "West's dad likes to organize all of my things."

Something about this wasn't adding up. "What kinds of things?"

She backed up a step. "Would you like to see?"

Gidget must have thought West's mom was inviting her inside because she trotted right into the kitchen and headed for the living room.

"I'm sorry." I followed after Gidget. As soon as I crossed the threshold to the living room, the smell of mildew and dust hit me. It smelled ten times worse than the Hilmer Library ever had. And I couldn't make sense of what I was seeing. Boxes upon boxes were stacked everywhere. And I do mean everywhere. They were stacked floor to ceiling leaving a small passage to the front door. If there was furniture in the living room, it was no longer visible.

Poor West. All the times I'd teased him about being a

neat freak...and all his comments about dust and mildew and not wanting to bring anything into his house...it all made tragic sense now. Tears pricked my eyes.

"These are my things." West's mom sounded so proud.

I couldn't look at her. Swallowing over the lump in my throat, I focused on Gidget. "Wow. You have a lot of stuff." I needed to get out of there. Quickly.

"I've been collecting for years."

I did my best to keep a happy expression on my face. Grabbing Gidget's collar, I turned to head back toward the kitchen. His mom stood there with a dreamy expression on her face, like her house was full of rare treasures. "I can see that. I better get Gidget out of here before she accidentally knocks over your boxes."

"Oh...that's probably a good idea." She headed back to the kitchen.

I followed leading Gidget back out the patio door. "It was nice meeting you," I said.

"You, too." She looked past me. "Oh, hello, West."

My stomach dropped to my shoes. West stood there, pale faced, with his fists clenched.

Chapter Thirty-Five

All I could do was stand there and stare, trying to make sense of the scene unfolding in front of me. Nina stood there talking to my mom. Not only that, she was coming out of my house. She'd been in the house. She'd seen the boxes. She knew. "Nina, what are you doing?"

"Your mom asked to pet Gidget," she said.

Everything I'd been hiding for so long was exposed. The look of pity on Nina's face made me want to punch something.

"Aren't you proud of me?" my mom said. "I spoke to someone."

She was oblivious to the panic running through my veins like ice water. Was this what I wanted, for her to talk to people? I wasn't sure anymore. To head off any type of meltdown, I nodded. "I'm proud of you. You should talk to people."

"Gidget is so sweet," my mom said. "And I like Nina, too."

Nina laughed, but it sounded forced.

"Mom, why don't you start a pot of coffee while I walk

Nina back to her house?"

"Okay, dear." She went back into the house and shut the door.

"West?" Nina came toward me. "Are you okay?"

"Not here." I couldn't risk my mom overhearing. I put my arm on Nina's shoulder and guided her back to her yard. My head was pounding. When we reached the picnic table I sat. Now what?

"It's okay," Nina said.

The absurdity of her statement made me laugh. "No. It's not. And what in the hell did you think you were doing going over there? I told you never to bother my mother. I told you not to disturb her. She's sick."

Nina sucked in a breath. "I was trying to be kind. She waved me over. She wanted to pet Gidget. And you don't get to be mad at me because I never lied to you like you have lied to me."

"I lied to you? When?"

She leaned in. "You made me think your mom was sick, like she had cancer or something. She's not sick at all."

If only that were true. "She's not? Do you seriously think stacking boxes floor to ceiling throughout the entire house is the act of a healthy person?"

"No. But you could have told me about your mom and her issues," Nina said. "I told you everything."

"Your drama is in the past," I said. "And mine is happening right now. Besides, I didn't lie to you; I just didn't tell you the whole truth."

"That's the same thing," she said.

"It's not." I heard the sound of my dad's Humvee pulling up the drive. Time for damage control. "I don't have time for this. I have to go."

I ran to the back door and entered the kitchen to find my mom sitting at the table drinking coffee like nothing was wrong, like our entire lives weren't about to come crashing down. "You can't tell Dad about Nina," I said.

She waved my concerns away. "I don't know what you're so worried about."

My dad came into the house carrying a bucket of KFC. He looked at her face and then at mine. "What did I miss?"

My mom launched into her tale about talking to Nina and petting Gidget. Thankfully, she didn't mention that Nina had been in the house. My father listened and smiled in all the right places, but the smile appeared strained. "That's nice, honey." He turned away from us and grabbed plates, knives, and forks. Then he set out the chicken, mashed potatoes, and green beans.

He filled a plate and took a seat. I grabbed some food and sat at the table, eating it mechanically, waiting for all hell to break loose.

"West was worried you'd be mad about Nina," my mom said.

I wanted to lay my head on the table. Why couldn't she do one simple thing I asked?

"If talking to her made you happy"—he seemed to be measuring his words before saying them—"then that's okay. You just can't let anyone in the house."

I gripped my fork tight and prayed my mom had the good sense to keep the rest of the story to herself.

"Too late." She laughed. "Gidget ran in and Nina came after her. I showed her the boxes in the living room. She was impressed with my collection."

Oh, God.

"I'm sure she was." My dad ate his food like he wasn't planning to end my life, but I'm pretty sure he was.

After dinner, I retreated to my room. How was I supposed to deal with this situation? Nina was mad because she thought I lied. My dad wasn't happy about Nina knowing our secret. My mentally ill mom thought everything was wonderful.

My cell beeped. It was from Nina. *Can we talk?*

No. We couldn't, because I had no idea what to say. How in the hell could I explain my mom and her bizarre ways? I ignored the message.

A knock sounded on my door, and then my dad pushed it open. I never understood why he knocked if he was going to barge right in anyway.

"What happened with Nina today," he said, "that wasn't good."

"I know." What else did he expect me to say?

"Make sure it doesn't happen again."

How in the hell was I supposed to make sure Nina never came over? Maybe I could diffuse the situation. "This happened because Mom wanted to see the dog," I said. "Not because she wanted to talk to Nina."

"That may be what your mother claims, but she never would've called Nina over if you weren't dating her. Just make sure Nina understands that I will kick her family out if she does anything to harm or upset your mother."

"Nina would never—"

"Your mother is more important than the rental income. I will kick Nina and her family out and let your mom fill that house with boxes if you don't take care of this situation. Do you understand?"

Afraid of what might come out of my mouth, I just nodded.

"All right then." My dad left, slamming the door behind him.

Why did he have to be so unreasonable? Nina would never do anything to hurt my mom. Someone, like me or my father, was more likely to be hurt due to the fire hazard our house had become. Death by storage container landslide wasn't out of the question either. One thing I knew for sure, I couldn't wait to get out of this crazy house.

Chapter Thirty-Six

NINA

Not being able to tell anyone about the insanity at West's house was making me crazy. Normally, I told Lisa everything, but I knew I couldn't share this. Why wasn't West responding to my text? Maybe he was eating dinner.

I felt so sorry for him and for his mom. She seemed like a lost child, rather than a parent. None of that made up for the fact that he'd lied to me. I'd bared my soul about my dad, and he'd smiled and nodded, listening to my sob story. Why hadn't he told me the truth? Didn't he trust me? I was his girlfriend.

This had been one hell of a Monday. I texted West again. No response. I didn't want to annoy him, but I needed some sort of answer. Maybe him not calling me back was his response. Or maybe he was trying to cope with the fact that I knew the truth about his mom.

The next morning after I got ready for school, I checked the driveway. West sat in his car, reading. Or pretending to read. Maybe that was how he avoided conversation.

I walked out and climbed in, putting on my seat belt in silence, waiting for him to say something. He started the car and drove. Still nothing.

"You never texted me back."

"Sorry." His voice sounded oddly flat.

"How's your mom?" I asked.

"Fine."

Was this One-Word-Answer Day? "And your dad?"

"Not fine."

Okay we'd moved up to two words. "Anything you'd like to get off your chest?"

"No."

Okay. Time to jump in and get the awkwardness out of the way. "I understand you're upset, but I didn't do anything wrong."

"I told you never to go to my house," he said. "And you did."

"Only because your mom waved me over." How did he not understand this? "Besides, you saw her. Gidget made her happy."

"The cardboard tubes from paper towel rolls make her happy. Five-year-old junk mail makes her happy. Every straw that's ever been used in our house, which she keeps in Ziploc bags, makes her happy."

Oh my God. "She keeps used straws?"

"Yes. And the bags eventually fill up with mold. And my father lets her keep them in Rubbermaid storage containers in their bedroom because he loves her and doesn't want to upset her."

Holy crap. That was beyond disturbing. "Can't she go see a counselor?"

"She's been to five. None of them made any difference."

He sounded so defeated. "I'm sorry."

"Me, too. It doesn't make any difference though, does it?"

After that, there wasn't much to say. We walked through the parking lot, but he didn't hold my hand. He didn't kiss me at my locker. He walked off in a daze like he was an emotionless robot.

"What's up with West?" Lisa asked.

I wanted to tell her about his mom, but if I did, and he found out about it, he'd never forgive me. So I went with the simplest explanation. "Family problems."

"That stinks. Maybe he should talk to my mom."

That gave me an idea. "If I talked to your mom about him, would she offer suggestions? Tell me things I could maybe do to help?"

"I don't think it works that way. You can only talk about your own issues."

"Crap."

West didn't join me at lunch, but he did approach every table to hand out stacks of fliers. Every table but ours.

Lisa stood and went over to another table and nabbed a flier for us. She brought it back to our table and held the flier so I could read it, too. It made a compelling case, listing the amount of items the average recycling center saved from landfills every year. There was also an ad for Paula's Pizza Pies, which instructed people to sign the petition on the bulletin board by the front office if they wanted to be entered into a drawing for a family dinner consisting of pizza, a salad, and breadsticks.

"We may need to up our game," Lisa said.

"How?" I asked. "Get your mom to offer a free counseling session?"

She laughed. "*Uhm*...no. We could offer some fancy bookmarks or a book light."

"A bookworm-themed gift basket?" That might work.

"We could add a coffee cup and some cocoa to round it out."

"Not to be a downer, but I'm not sure it's worth the effort. And what happens if people sign both petitions?" she asked.

"Good question. As with everything else going on in my life, I have no answers." Although I did have one answer. I now knew why West was so passionate about turning the library into a recycling center. How could he live in that house? All those boxes stacked on top of each other had to be a safety hazard and a fire hazard, not to mention a health hazard.

Why wasn't there any way to help his mom? The look on her face when she'd talked about her collection had been almost eerie. She believed those boxes of crap—moldy straws and God knows what else—were treasures worth keeping. If someone I loved started acting like that, I'd want to stage an intervention with a Dumpster.

"Earth to Nina." Lisa stood holding her backpack. "Time for class."

"Sorry."

"What were you thinking about?" she asked.

"I know why West is crabby, but I don't know how to help."

After school, he was no better. When he pulled the car into the driveway and parked, I hoped he'd want to talk. He exited the vehicle. I scrambled out and after him.

"Hey, why don't you come to my house for dinner tonight."

He kept walking. "No thanks," he said without turning around.

Ugh. Did he need time to pout? Was that it? His life wasn't any different today than it was yesterday. I knew the truth about his family, which he should have told me in the first place. If anyone had a right to pout it was me. But I was trying to be the levelheaded one in this situation. Because one of us had to be. If we both sulked, life would never go back to normal.

While I understood why he was upset, I didn't understand why he was shutting me out. In times of trouble, you were supposed to turn to the people who cared about you, not run away from them. And I did care about West. If it was so easy for him to shut me out, did he care about me?

I could ask him...if I followed him to his house and knocked on the back door, but I doubt he'd respond positively to that maneuver. So, I headed to my house and to the one person I knew would always be happy to see me. Gidget bounded up to greet me in her usual ecstatic fashion, spreading joy and fur. I hugged her and rubbed her ears.

"Want some banana bread?" I asked.

She did her excited food dance and followed me to the kitchen. With the dog's help, I finished off the third of a loaf that was left. Then I retrieved one of the many loaves my mom had put in the freezer and set it on the counter to defrost. Wait a minute. I set a second one on the counter and toyed with the idea of taking it to West's mom. Maybe I could give it to West, now that I knew germs weren't an issue.

I was still pissed about him lying to me, but I understood why he did it. Instead of trying to cover up something he'd done, he was trying to protect his mom.

Chapter Thirty-Seven

"How's Nina?" my mom asked when I came in the patio doors.

"Fine." I headed to the coffee maker and started a pot of French roast. Then I grabbed the peanut butter, jelly, and bread per our normal after-school tradition.

"We should ask her over for dinner," my mom said.

I grabbed a knife from the utensil drawer and started making sandwiches, ignoring her absurd statement.

"West, did you hear me?" she said.

"Yes. It's not a good idea. Dad is still mad that she was in the house."

"Oh, he's not mad," she said.

I finished making the sandwiches and put everything away before pouring two cups of coffee and joining her at the table. "If he's not mad, then why did he threaten to evict Nina's family?"

She laughed. "He was joking."

"No. He wasn't. He doesn't want anyone in the house but us." I sipped my coffee and prayed for patience.

"Why would you think that?" she asked.

I closed my eyes. Did we really need to have this conversation again? "I know you see the world differently, but I need you to listen to me. We can't invite anyone into the house." What could I offer as a compromise? "You can go out onto the patio if you want, but you can't let anyone in here. There are too many boxes. They could fall on someone. People could get hurt."

"Oh...well maybe your father should work at making them safer."

I had to bite my tongue to keep from suggesting she get rid of some of the useless garbage she collected instead. Why wouldn't she let this thing with Nina go? There was only one solution. "I didn't want to tell you this, but you shouldn't ask Nina to come over for dinner because I'm going to break up with her."

"What?" She set her coffee down and reached across the table to touch my hand "Why?"

Why? Because she was a complication I didn't need in my life. Because being close to anyone never worked out. Because if I didn't she'd probably be evicted. "Things just aren't working out," I said.

"I'm sorry. I thought she was nice."

I nodded and ate my sandwich. Then I went to my room and stared at the ceiling. Breaking up with Nina was the only logical solution. It's not like she was the only girl on the planet. If I ended things between us, would she keep my secret? My gut said yes. And that was all that mattered. Sort of.

Did I want to end things with her? No, but there wasn't another option that would keep my mom from asking Nina to come over. If only my mom would listen to common sense, but common sense had vanished from her head a long time ago.

Feeling restless, I headed outside to the barbecue court. There was a foil-wrapped package on top of the grill. What was that about?

I picked it up and read the attached note. *Banana Bread: Reheat in the oven at 350 degrees for ten minutes.* Why had Nina left this for me? Probably because she knew my mom never baked, and she seemed to show love through food.

Holy hell. Did I just think that? Love? Nina wasn't in love with me. I certainly wasn't in love with her. She was fun to hang around, and, despite what I'd said before, it was convenient to have the girl I was dating live next door. Of course, it was also a terrible idea, due to my dad compulsively trying to hide the fact that my mom was a hoarder.

"I see you found the banana bread." Nina practically materialized in front of me.

I jerked backward. "Where'd you come from?"

"Hello. I'm Nina. I live next door." She grinned like she was making a joke.

"Not funny," I said.

"Okay then." She rocked back on her heels. "I saw you come out here, so I followed."

For some reason, that ticked me off. "You just assumed you'd be welcome."

She stared at me for a moment like I'd spoken a foreign language.

"I'm sorry," she said. "Did you want to be alone?"

And here was my opening. "I do. As a matter of fact, this whole couple thing isn't working for me. You should plan to drive yourself to school tomorrow."

"Excuse me?"

"I'm sorry. Was I unclear?" I moved toward her and spoke more slowly. "Let me break it down for you. We're done. It's over. Go away."

She blinked and looked at me. "I know you're upset about your mom, but you don't mean that."

"I do." I couldn't let her argue her way out of this. So I said the one thing I knew she'd never forgive me for. "You living next door is convenient, but this whole neighbors-with-benefits thing has turned out to be more trouble than it's worth."

She sucked in a breath, turned around, and ran back to her house.

And that was that.

Chapter Thirty-Eight

NINA

I fled back to my house, yanked open the patio door, and slammed it shut behind me. Gidget came running. I led her to the couch where she jumped up beside me. Hugging her, I tried to make sense of what had just happened. West's hateful words replayed in my head. Had he really meant that? I was convenient? That's why he was with me?

The cynical part of my brain laughed and pointed out the obvious. Why would he put forth the effort to meet a girl he liked if there was one next door who was willing to sneak off to a shed and make out with him? How could I have been so naive…so stupid?

My eyes burned, and a cold, dull ache radiated through my bones. I never should have trusted him. I could have sworn he liked me, cared about me. If he had, he couldn't just end things and walk away from me, right?

Since he had done exactly that, it meant he'd never actually cared. The realization slammed into my chest, making it hard to take a full breath. I wanted to curl up in a ball. Instead, I hugged Gidget and let the angry tears flow.

Gidget whined and licked my face.

"You're the best dog." She yodeled in agreement and cuddled closer, providing furry warmth and unconditional love.

Screw West. I didn't need him. Right now his biggest punishment was he would get exactly what he wanted—to be alone with a crazy hoarding mom and an almost-as-crazy OCD dad.

Besides, I didn't need him. I had a dog. And dogs were far more loyal than men. Hadn't my own father proven that?

Once I was cried out, I called Lisa.

"I can't believe he broke up with you. Did he say why?"

"No." I sniffled. I couldn't tell her what he'd said. It was too painful and humiliating.

"What a jackass. Is there anything I can do to help?" she asked.

When I was thoroughly stressed out, the only thing that helped me cope were books. "I need something to help me ignore reality. Want to run to the bookstore?"

"Sure. I'll pick you up in twenty minutes."

I ran to the bathroom and checked the mirror. Wow. Waterproof mascara, my ass. It looked like I'd cried black paint. I washed my face and didn't bother applying any new makeup.

I left a note on the kitchen table telling my mom where I'd gone. Maybe Lisa and I would eat cookies from the bookstore cafe for dinner. That was the only thing that sounded good right now.

• • •

Waking up Tuesday morning was extra sucky. In retrospect,

staying up until two in the morning to finish my book had not been a smart plan, but I had needed a happily ever after, even if it was fictional. The three cookies I had for dinner probably hadn't helped, either.

To top it off, I'd forgotten to reset my alarm to a reasonable human time of the morning, so I woke up at the stupid early time I'd been waking up to ride with West. But I wasn't riding with West, because he was an emotionally stunted idiot. So I spied out the window as he climbed into his car and backed down the driveway without so much as a glance in my direction.

"Are you okay?" my mom asked.

I gave her a look worthy of her dumb question.

"You know what I mean," she said. "Is there anything I can do?"

"No." Part of me wanted to stay home and pout, while the other half wanted to go to school to show West I was fine without him. "Guys suck."

"Yes, yes they do." She gave me a quick hug.

"Cole isn't a jerk." Jason called out from the kitchen.

"But now you're being one," I yelled back.

"You'll be fine," my mom said. "Because you have me and Gidget and Jason and Lisa. You're luckier than West. Remember that."

Was this how my mom had coped with my dad's betrayal? "Thanks, Mom. I better go."

The first thing I noticed when I walked into school was the fresh round of recycling posters taped all over the hallways. Wherever one of my KEEP THE HILMER LIBRARY OPEN posters hung, one of West's was displayed right next to it. That was rude. He should find his own spots to hang posters.

I had to walk past West's locker to reach mine. Charlie made eye contact with me and gave a quick nod. I nodded back. West pretended I was invisible, which made my stomach ache. Acting like it didn't bother me, I kept walking.

At my locker, I noticed the gossip who'd asked me about West a few weeks ago. She sidled closer as I worked the combination lock.

"Can I help you?" I asked.

"Is it true?" she asked. "Did you and West break up?"

"We did," I said, keeping my tone even, like it wasn't a big deal.

"Sorry about that," she said.

Sure she was. I nodded and went back to organizing my books. Lisa showed up a few minutes later.

"Any problems so far this morning?" she asked.

"Besides the burning desire to kick West in the balls? No."

She pulled a flat bakery bag from her backpack. "Just in case you needed more cookies."

I was pretty much cookied out, but I took the bag. "Thanks. Did you notice how pro-recycling signs popped up next to all of our save the library signs?"

"Yes. That's sort of rude."

"My thoughts exactly. So what are we going to do about it?" I asked.

"We could accidentally rip them off the walls," she suggested.

"I don't have a better idea," I said. "But we probably shouldn't do that."

By lunch, all I wanted to do was go home and go to sleep.

Matt approached our table and sat down. "I don't know what happened between you two, but West is a miserable SOB today. He's barely speaking to us."

"Good," Lisa said. "He broke up with Nina. He deserves to be miserable."

Matt frowned. "*Huh*...from the way he's acting, I would have thought it was the other way around."

"Nope," I said. "This is all his doing. Feel free to punch him if the opportunity arises."

He nodded and walked off.

• • •

WEST

Matt and Charlie waited for me by my car after school. I don't know what they had in mind, but I was not in the mood to go anywhere or deal with anyone. "What's up?" I asked.

"That's what we wanted to ask you," Matt said.

"Yeah," Charlie chimed in. "Why are you in such a foul mood?"

I didn't owe either of them an explanation, but I couldn't really talk to anyone else about this. Glancing around to make sure no one was close enough to overhear, I said, "My mom spoke to Nina and let her in the house."

"That's good, right?" Matt said.

I stared at him, waiting for him to get a freaking clue.

"Or not," Charlie said. "Because of your mom's collection."

"My dad read me the riot act. I told Nina when we started dating that she could never come over to my house and bother my mom, and she did it anyway. The end." And with that, I got in my car. There was nothing left to discuss.

• • •

Wednesday morning when I walked to my locker, I knew something was up. Matt and Charlie stood nearby with their heads together like they were plotting something. As I worked the combination lock, they came to stand on either side of me.

"Whatever it is, the answer is no." I didn't like it when they pulled the twin card and ganged up on me.

"Crab ass." Matt leaned against his locker. "You don't even know what we were going to say."

"Fine. Talk."

"You didn't have to break up with Nina," Charlie said. "She knows your secret. You could be honest with her."

"That's not the point," I said.

"Then what is the point?" Matt asked. "Making yourself miserable?"

I didn't bother answering. I just headed off to homeroom. Matt and Charlie had no right to judge me. They didn't live in my house. They didn't know what it was like to deal with crazy twenty-four hours a day. And not just my mom's craziness, my dad was also nuts in his own antisocial, OCD way. And yes, Nina knew about them, but that didn't make the situation okay; it made it worse. When I was out of the house I could pretend my life was normal. Having Nina know meant I couldn't pretend anymore. The crazy would always be there staring me in the face. I was better off dating a girl who lived across town, someone who'd never know about my family. Someone who didn't look at me with pity.

• • •

Wednesday, Thursday, and Friday all rolled into one big ball of shittiness. I avoided talking to everyone because Matt and Charlie kept prying, and my mom wouldn't stop asking about Nina.

My dad was the only person who seemed happy.

Saturday afternoon, I went for a drive to clear my head.

My life was fine. I didn't need a girlfriend, especially one who lived next door to me who could bring everything crashing down around me at any moment.

I only had three months left of school. Time to focus on which college I wanted to attend. I'd been accepted by several with good engineering programs and was still trying to make up my mind. Maybe I'd pick the one farthest away. My dad could cater to my mom's craziness all he wanted, while I lived a normal life someplace else.

With no plan in mind, I drove downtown near the barbeque place where Nina and I had eaten. I Googled the restaurant's phone number, ordered the family special as carryout, and waited in the parking lot for it to be ready. Because it's not like I had someone at home cooking me dinner.

Couples walked up and down the street holding hands, looking in the stupid store windows. All the girls were smiling. Most of the guys didn't seem unhappy, but I could tell this wasn't their favorite activity. I was glad not to be one of those guys who had to pretend to be interested in window displays, even though Nina and I had had a good time.

When twenty minutes had passed, I headed over to the restaurant to pick up my food. On the drive home, I ate fries straight from the bag. They weren't as good as I remembered.

At home, I found my mom and dad eating pizza in the kitchen. I held up my bag of carryout. "I picked up barbecue, if you want some."

"Maybe later," my dad said.

I fixed a plate and sat at the table.

"Are you feeling any better?" my mom asked.

It took me a moment to realize she was speaking to me. "I'm fine."

"No. You're not," my dad said. "What's wrong?"

I set my fork down. Resentment rose up inside me.

"Nothing's wrong. I made sure Nina wouldn't be a problem anymore, just like you told me to."

"Why would she be a problem?" my mom asked.

I let my dad field that question since he was the one who'd set this ball in motion, but he didn't say anything. Fine. "Dad didn't want Nina over here, and you wouldn't stop asking about her, so I did what I had to do. I broke up with her."

My dad looked at me like I'd said something that didn't make sense.

"I don't know why you look surprised," I said. "Everything I do—keeping to myself, only being friends with Matt and Charlie, never getting too close to anyone, living like a freaking hermit—is to keep our family secret."

My dad shook his head. "I never asked you to do that. I thought you were like me, that you preferred to keep to yourself."

"No." I wanted to shout at him, but I didn't have the energy. "I put my entire life on hold to try and keep the peace around here." I sank down in my chair. I thought confessing this might make me feel better, but it just felt like I had fallen deeper into a hole of my own making. This was all too much.

"I don't understand why Nina can't come over," my mom said.

I loved my mother, but I'd reached my limit. "How we live isn't normal. Your collection…all of these boxes stacked floor to ceiling is not normal. Anyone who came into the house—"

"West, that's enough!" my dad shouted.

"Why?" I was on a roll. "Why can't we talk about it? Mom is a hoarder. It's a fact. Not naming the problem won't make it go away."

"Pointing it out doesn't make it any better either." My dad reached across the table to hold my mom's hand. He looked at her as he spoke. "This isn't your fault."

My mom stared uncomprehending at me and then at my

dad. "I don't understand, but if I stop asking about Nina, will that make it better?"

"Nothing will make this better." I stood and stalked off to my room. Lying in bed, I rubbed my temples hoping to make my pounding headache go away.

My bedroom door swung open.

"What?" I sat up, expecting to see my father.

My mom stood there ringing her hands. "Go talk to Nina. She made you happy. Your father and I want you to be happy."

"It's too late for that."

"It's never too late," she said. "Go make things right."

"I'm not sure I can." I'd said some unforgivable things.

"Think about it." My mom left, closing the door behind her.

It was a little late for motherly concern and advice. Could I make this right after what I'd said? The truth was, even though Nina might make my life more difficult, I had been happier with her than without her. Was that how my dad felt about my mom? Not that I planned to propose marriage to Nina, but I wanted her back in my life. After the way I'd broken things off with her, I needed to come up with a good argument to win her back. First step: talking to her.

Chapter Thirty-Nine

I went back into the now empty kitchen and looked out the window toward Nina's backyard. She was seated at the picnic table with her back to my house. Her brother, Jason, was nowhere to be seen, but her mom sat across from her. Gidget lay in the grass chewing on a rawhide bone.

What could I say to her? I had no idea. All I could do was try. I headed out the back door. Nina's mom saw me coming. Her eyebrows shot up, which clued Nina in.

She turned around, spotted me, and frowned. "What do you want?"

"I wanted to talk to you."

"I'm a little busy now." Nina indicated the game of Life she and her mom were playing.

"Who's winning?" I asked.

"None of your damn business," Nina replied, and turned back around.

Okay then. I knew this wouldn't be simple, but I was

already over here, and I wasn't giving up without a fight, so I sat down next to her.

"No one invited you to sit," she said.

"I know you're mad," I started in. "And you have every right to be."

"Nope. Not mad. I might be profoundly pissed off, hateful, and fantasizing about kicking you in the balls, but I wouldn't say I'm mad."

"Okay. I deserve that. The terrible things I said when I broke up with you, I didn't mean them. I said them on purpose to drive you away."

"Mission accomplished," she shot back. "Anything else you want to share before you *Go Away*?"

I got it. She was throwing my words back in my face. Time to cut to the chase. "Breaking up with you was the only way I could keep my mom from inviting you to dinner."

"Wait a minute," Nina's mom said. "I thought you said your mom was sick and couldn't have visitors."

"He lied," Nina said.

"I didn't lie. My mom *is* ill," I said. "But it's not her immune system that's the problem. She's mentally fragile, so my dad is overprotective of her. If my mom had invited Nina to dinner, my dad would have followed through on his threat to evict you."

"What the hell?" Nina said. "That's why you broke up with me?"

I nodded.

"Did you ever think you could have talked to me about this, instead of acting like the biggest jerk on the planet?"

"You don't understand. My mom is not rational. She doesn't back down from an idea once it's in her head. My dad literally threatened to kick you out and let my mom fill the house with more of her crazy collection. Breaking up with you seemed like the only solution."

"Why can't Nina eat dinner at your house?" her mom asked.

"I haven't seen our dining room table in more than three years. I guess it's still in there somewhere, but it's buried under boxes of useless crap my mom collects. My dad loves her, and therapy didn't help, so he puts all of her things in storage boxes. My entire house is floor-to-ceiling boxes, and my dad doesn't want anyone to know, so I've been telling people that my mom is ill for years."

"Oh...wow." Her mom frowned. "I'll go inside and let you two talk."

After her mom left, I scooted closer to Nina. "I swear you weren't just convenient. Can you give me a second chance?"

"If this is supposed to be an apology, it's not working," Nina said. "Rather than telling me the truth, like you said you would, you threw my worst fear in my face. You made me feel worthless, just like my father did."

"I'm sorry." I reached for her hand, but she yanked it away.

"Don't touch me."

Well, this was a spectacular failure. "If you ever want to talk, you know where to find me." I stood and walked toward my house, hoping she'd call me back. Of course, that didn't happen. Apparently, there are some things an apology can't fix.

・・・

NINA

My mom must have been hovering by the patio doors, because she came back outside as soon as West left. "I take it that didn't go well."

"No," I said.

"So West's dad is the mentally healthier parent?" my

mom asked. "Poor West."

"Right. Poor West." I spun the spinner with a little too much gusto, and it took forever to land on a number. I moved my game piece three spaces. "He should have told me the truth."

"You're right," my mom said. "But sometimes being right isn't everything. Sometimes you need to think about what makes you happy."

I froze. "If you're trying to tell me you're getting back together with Dad, I swear to God I'm moving in with Lisa."

"What? No. Never. What your dad did was selfish and wrong, not to mention illegal. What West did was stupid and shortsighted and immature. You're the only one who can decide if it's forgivable."

Later that night I called Lisa and relayed the interaction with West and what my mom said. "And honestly, there's only so much time and effort I'm willing to put into any relationship," I said. "And I'm not sure West is worth the trouble."

"So you think you've reached the end of your emotional budget?" Lisa asked. "Where his issues aren't worth the emotional investment?"

"Maybe. Is that something your mom tells people when she's counseling them?"

"Yes."

"It makes sense to have an emotional boyfriend budget. Some sort of scale to decide if the good outweighs the bad. If you are better off with or without a guy." I pulled at a thread on the sleeve of my sweatshirt and the hem unraveled. "Crap." West had warned me about that. Was this some sign from the universe that I needed to leave well enough alone or that I needed to hear West out? Or...it could just be an old shirt with weakened thread.

"So what are you going to do?" Lisa asked.

"I have no idea. Part of me wants to hear him out. Part of me wants to break the mirrors off of his Fusion with a baseball bat."

She laughed. "Let me know if I need to come play lookout so you won't get caught."

After hanging up with Lisa, I thought about West. He claimed he didn't mean what he'd said. Oh, how I wanted to believe that. Did I want to give another chance to a guy who'd hurt me on purpose, even if it was to protect his mom? I didn't know. And yes, he'd been trying to keep me from being evicted, but all of this pain could have been avoided if he'd just told me the truth. But he hadn't. And that was the real problem.

$$\bullet \bullet \bullet$$

WEST

Sunday night, I sat out on my barbecue court, burning sticks and charcoal in the grill. I'd given up on bringing paper out here to burn. If my dad didn't care about five-year-old mildew-stained mail, then why should I give a shit?

I listened, hoping I might hear Gidget running and barking. Maybe she'd lead Nina out here to me so I could try pleading my case again. Even though I'd eaten dinner, my gut felt cold and empty. God, I was pathetic. She was just a girl. There were other girls out there. A small voice in my head pointed out that the other girls probably wouldn't try to feed me every time I came over or give me loaves of homemade banana bread. They wouldn't hide out with me during rainstorms reading *Harry Potter* out loud. Nina was different. I'd never met a girl like her before, and I probably never would again.

My cell buzzed. I checked the text and was slightly

disappointed when I saw it was from Charlie. He and Matt were going to grab something to eat if I wanted to meet them. I texted back a quick *No thanks*, and then stared at my phone, willing Nina to text me. Of course, that didn't happen. There had to be something I could do to show her how sorry I was.

• • •

Monday morning, Mr. Grant made the official announcement that the pro-recycling petition had more signatures than the one to keep the library open. The political powers-that-be felt the same say, so the Hilmer Library would become a recycling center, which meant people would have to drive forty minutes to the library, if they wanted to borrow books. That was one more reason for Nina to be mad at me, even though I couldn't do anything to make that situation better.

At lunch, I Googled traveling libraries to see if there were any groups who shuttled books around to towns who didn't have their own libraries. There were, but Greenbrier didn't qualify for services. There had to be something else I could do. And then I had an idea.

I stayed after school so I could talk to Mr. Grant. Since his brother was donating the manpower to rehab the interior of the Hilmer building, turning it into a glorified warehouse, maybe we could alter the plans just a little bit. I had an idea that might make Nina and the other library ladies happy.

Mr. Grant listened to me, and then he smiled. "I'm proud of you for thinking of this. It's such a simple concept, and it will make two groups of people happy. Good job."

"Thanks." I only hoped it would be enough to make Nina give me another chance.

"I'll let my brother know that you'll come by after school tomorrow to help set things up."

There...now I had a plan. I didn't know if it would be

enough for Nina to forgive me, and I'd need to enlist some help if I was going to make this happen. I shared my plan with Matt and Charlie at lunch.

"That's not a bad idea," Matt said. "I don't know if it will win Nina back, but it's a good start."

"I might need your help getting Nina to the right place at the right time. Can you talk to Lisa about this, because I don't think she'll listen to me."

Matt nodded. "I can do that."

Three days later, after school, I waited outside the recycling center for Nina and Lisa to arrive.

Matt texted me when the girls were on their way.

I stood off to the side of the sign I'd just finished hanging. I heard Nina before I saw her come around the corner of the building.

"I don't know why you'd think I'd want to see this stupid recycling center," she griped.

"Just keep moving," Lisa said.

Nina came around the corner, spotted me, and then noticed the sign. "Hilmer Book Recycling Center? What's this?"

"It's a free library." I gestured that she should go through the door.

She seemed unsure, but she entered the building. I followed and then watched as she scanned the small room.

I pointed at the half-full bookshelves. "People can donate books they no longer want and pick up a different book to take home." I pointed at the bulletin boards on the wall labeled *Book Reviews* and *Book Requests*. "People can leave reviews recommending a book or ask if anyone has seen a copy of a book they want. And that corner over there"—I pointed to an old brown leather couch my uncle had donated—"is for people who want to hang out here and read." The sign above the couch read: Nina's Book Nook, and a there was a small bookshelf next to it featuring a hard-backed boxed set of *Harry Potter.*

Nina turned in a circle and took everything in.

My heart beat faster in my chest. *Will this work?*

. . .

NINA

West had done this for me? It was a fantastic idea. "I like it. It's a great idea. Good job."

His smile faltered. "Thanks."

Did he think this made up for the terrible things he'd said? I wasn't sure if it did. Still, he'd put a lot of effort into this place. I don't think he would have done that if he didn't care about me.

"When did you decide to do this?" I asked.

"After I talked to you in your backyard and realized a simple apology wasn't going to cut it," he said. "I was hoping you'd see it as a peace offering and maybe you'd give me another chance."

"Why do you want another chance?" I asked.

"You're going to make me argue my case about why we should get back together, aren't you?" he asked.

I nodded. "Got it in one."

"Fine." He reached for my hand, and I let him lace his fingers through mine. Warmth radiated from his touch. "My house is a very stressful place. The only time I've been happy lately is when I'm with you. You make my world better. And I'd want to be with you even if you didn't live next door."

Should I believe him? He seemed sincere.

"I think this is one of those hugging moments," West said, pulling me closer until we were toe-to-toe.

"It is?" I asked.

"Yes," he said. "I'm hoping it will be followed by a kissing moment, but that's up to you."

"How's it going in there?" Lisa called out as she peeked around the doorframe.

"We're dating again," West said.

"Cool. I'm out of here. You can give Nina a ride home."

Lisa took off, and I looked at West. "Funny, I don't remember agreeing to date you."

"Too late." He grinned like he was quite proud of himself. "I said it. You didn't argue. Lisa heard it. So now we have to date; otherwise, you lied to your best friend."

"You think you're so smart," I said, "don't you?"

"With the recent exception of being a total dumb-ass... yes, I'm smart enough to know a good thing when I see it, and this time I'm not letting go."

"And next time there's a problem you'll talk to me rather than push me away?"

"Yes. And in case you haven't figured it out yet," he said, "this is a kissing moment."

I grinned as his mouth came toward mine. He pulled me closer, and I leaned into him, enjoying the sensation of being wrapped in his arms. It felt right. It felt like I was where I belonged. I knew West and I wouldn't always agree on everything. We were bound to have some disagreements, but as long as he took the time to talk to me, everything should be all right.

When the kiss ended, I smiled up at him. "So...I hear there's some sort of Spring Fling dance coming up."

"And you think dances are stupid, so we're not going," he said.

"No, I think I've changed my mind," I teased. "I want to go to a dance."

"We're not going to a dance because the only reason you're saying you want to go is to torment me," he said.

"Maybe, maybe not. But If I really wanted to go, would you take me?"

"Yes," he said. "As penance and because I want to make you happy."

"Thank you." I kissed him. "And don't worry, I don't actually want to go to the dance."

"No," he said. "I think you're right. We should go to the dance."

"But I don't want to go to the dance." *What is he trying to pull?*

"I know," he said. "Let's go grab some coffee, and we can talk about what you're going to wear to the dance."

"Yes to the coffee," I said. "And no to the dance." We walked out of the lending library, hand in hand. West continued his debate on why we should go to the dance. His argument became more outrageous, and he had me laughing by the time we made it to his car. Maybe this is what relationships were supposed to be about, finding someone who wanted to make you happy because you made them happy. Even though West had freaked out and messed up big time, he'd put effort into making things right.

A small voice in the back of my head pointed out that we'd both be heading off to college soon, but that didn't mean we couldn't enjoy the time we had. Who knew, if things went well, maybe we'd go away to school together. Rather than focusing on a pie-in-the-sky-happily-ever-after ending, I'd focus on living in the moment and being happy for now. Just because my dad had been a jerk didn't mean West would be. Neither of us were perfect. Being in love and caring about someone was kind of like sharing a driveway. Being close to someone, putting your emotions out there, left you vulnerable. And accidents, like ripping West's car mirror off, or getting into fights, were bound to happen, but most things were fixable, if you put effort into it.

Epilogue

NINA

West's dad hadn't been thrilled with the idea of a dual graduation party, but it made sense since we both wanted to use the backyard on the same Saturday. Plus my mom had agreed to take care of all the food, if he'd round up some more outdoor tables and chairs for the backyard.

The funny part was that he'd put all the seating on our side of the yard and blocked off his patio with two barbecue grills. He kept his back to all of us while he grilled hot dogs and hamburgers.

West's mom sat behind the barbecue barrier at the umbrella table on their patio talking to a woman who I thought was West's aunt.

"Looks like your mom is doing okay," I said to West, who sat next to me.

"As long as no one tries to get past the barbecue grill barrier, I think everything will be fine," he said. "I'm glad that she's coming outside and talking to people."

"Those are both good things," I said.

"I know. While things seem to be going well, I wanted to give you something." He pulled a small white box from his pocket. The kind that came from a jewelry store.

Crap. We'd said we weren't exchanging gifts. I hadn't bought him anything. I did a quick inventory of anything I might have tucked away in drawer that I could give him and came up empty. "I didn't get you anything," I confessed.

"This isn't a graduation present."

"It's not?" Curious, I opened the lid. A silver ring made of tiny hearts connected together like a chain was nestled inside. I plucked it out and slid it on my right ring finger. "It's beautiful. Thank you." Warmth filled my chest as I watched the light reflect off the ring. "Why isn't it a graduation present?"

"It's a promise ring. Even though we won't live next door to each other anymore, we'll still be together," he said.

"We're going away to the same college," I reminded him.

"I know, but we won't literally be living right next door to each other anymore. I'll have to hike across campus to meet you." He smiled. "Plus it should let any guys you run into know that you're taken."

"You're worried I'll find someone else who reads *Harry Potter*?" I teased.

"Maybe."

I leaned over and gave him a quick kiss. I saw blonde fur creeping across the yard, like Gidget was stalking something. She came to a stop by the grills and sat right next to West's dad.

I tensed, waiting for him to shoo her away. Instead, he patted her on the head, glanced around, and then he nudged one of the hotdogs off the edge of the grill into the grass. Gidget did her happy food dance, grabbed the hot dog and trotted off with it.

"Did you see that?" I asked West.

"My first explanation is invasion of the body snatchers," West said.

"I think Gidget won your dad over."

"She's kind of hard to resist," West said. "Despite the fact that she sheds more than the laws of physics should allow."

I checked around to see where my mom was. She'd been concerned that our guests and West's guests wouldn't mesh. The only people West's dad had invited were his cousin's family, which worked, since Matt and Charlie planned to have a party at their house tomorrow.

Steve, a guy my mom worked with who was five years younger than her, was sticking to her like glue. She didn't seem upset by that fact. She'd been smiling a lot more lately, and even though she didn't say they were dating, I'm pretty sure Steve thought they were.

All in all, things had turned out pretty good. West's mom might still be a hoarder, but she was coming out of the house and talking to people. That was a step in the right direction. My mom was happy. West and I were still together, and we were going to the same college in a few months. I hadn't picked the college because it was where he was going to school. I'd chosen it for their creative writing program, which was a happy coincidence—or maybe the universe had wanted both of us to see that the world was a better place than we thought it was.

Acknowledgments

I'd like to thank Erin Molta and Stacy Abrams for their editing expertise and the entire Entangled Publishing team for believing in my Boyfriends. I'd also like to thank my friends and family for their love and support.

About the Author

Chris Cannon is the award-winning author of the Going Down In Flames series and the Boyfriend Chronicles. She lives in Southern Illinois with her husband and several furry beasts.

She believes coffee is the Elixir of Life. Most evenings after work, you can find her sucking down caffeine and writing fire-breathing paranormal adventures or romantic comedies. You can find her online at www.chriscannonauthor.com.

Discover more of Entangled Teen Crush's books...

LOVE BETWEEN ENEMIES
a *Grad Night* novel by Molly Lee

Zoey Handler is ready to put an end to her decade-long rivalry with Gordon Meyers. They've traded top spot between valedictorian and salutatorian for years, but all that's over now. Right? But after a crazy graduation speech prank gets out of hand, suddenly their rivalry turns into all-out war. Time to make peace with a little friendly payback.

THE HEARTBREAK CURE
a novel by Amanda Ashby

After being dumped and humiliated over the summer, Cat Turner does what any sane girl would do. She asks bad boy Alex Locke to be her fake boyfriend and show the world that she's fine. Problem is, the more time she spends with Alex, the more she risks getting her heart broken. For real this time.

THE SWEETHEART SHAM
a *Southern Charmed* novel by Danielle Ellison

Georgia Ann Monroe knows a thing or two about secrets: she's been guarding the truth that her best friend Will is gay for years now. But what happens when a little white lie to protect him gets her into a fake relationship…and *then* Beau, the boy of her dreams, shows up? There's no way to come clean to Beau while still protecting Will. But bless their hearts, they live in Culler—where secrets always have a way of revealing themselves.

DARING THE BAD BOY
an *Endless Summer* novel by Monica Murphy

A session at summer camp is just what shy Annie McFarland needs to reinvent herself. Too bad her fear of water keeps her away from the lake, and her new crush Kyle. Enter Jacob Fazio—junior counselor, all-around bad boy, and most importantly: lifeguard. When a night of Truth or Dare gets him roped into teaching Annie how to swim, she begs him to also teach her how to snag Kyle. Late-night swim sessions turn into late-night kissing sessions…but there's more on the line than just their hearts. If they get caught, Jake's headed straight to juvie.

Made in the USA
Columbia, SC
28 September 2020

21396195R00138